HAUNTED GRAVE
AND
OTHER STORIES

HAUNTED GRAVE
AND
OTHER STORIES

Ezeiyoke Chukwunonso

Parallel Universe Publications

Eaters of Flesh first appeared in *Lost Tales from the Mountain (A Halloween Anthology)*, edited by Abigail Kern and Riley Guyer, Mountain Spring House, Indiana, 2014.
Game of Aids first appeared in *Emanations: 2+2= 5*, edited by Carter Kaplan, International Authors Publication, Brookline, Massachusetts, 2015
A Cursed City first appeared in *Emanations: Foray into Forever*, edited by Carter Kaplan, International Authors Publication, Brookline, Massachusetts, 2014
The Last Man Standing first appeared in *Future Lovercraft*, edited by Silvia Moreno-Garcia and Paula Stiles, Innsmouth Free Press, Canada, 2011

ISBN: 978-0-9935742-3-8
Parallel Universe Publications, 130 Union Road,
Oswaldtwistle, Lancashire, BB5 3DR, UK

TABLE OF CONTENTS

EATERS OF FLESH

"Your mum disappeared."

That was how Dad said it, as if he were cracking a joke about the crazy attitude of the Arsenal's football coach with his friends. I didn't even know when I stood up that I pushed my stainless steel plate away. The plate fell from the dining table, bouncing on the ground with a shrill sound. My ogbono soup spilled on the floor, staining the white tiles. My father held me by my shoulders with his rough hands and forced me back to my seat.

He leant against my seat, his eyes on my face. His glaring was unbearable so I took my eyes away from him and instead tried to concentrate on the white curtain in front of me. The curtain was used to demarcate our dining room from the parlour. It had a lot of hibiscus flowers on it, so I forced myself to count those flowers to numb my thoughts.

"Everything will be okay," he said with a voice now coated with seriousness. I knew he was only mocking me, or Mum.

*

I collected the key to Mum's room from Dad. I needed her memory like a junkie would need cocaine. For the first time over the past three years I had the prospect of seeing her room again. I was lucky to be the last of her two surviving sons to be weaned from her presence when the illness began to take too much of a toll on her. Anyway, Dad didn't see it as an illness. He said that it was her excessive religious involvement that caused her peril. He would always scream at her, "Religion is bondage, free yourself." But her friend Onyinye believed that it was a spiritual attack from her enemies, especially since the disorder began a day after her forty-fifth birthday when Dad had given her a Honda Jeep as a birthday gift. She said Mum's relatives, who envied Dad's love for her, had struck her with madness.

I opened the door. My eyes automatically went to the eastern side of the room where I saw her last. She had sat on the ground beside her bed with half of the bed sheet on the floor. A litany of her clothes and shoes were on the bed. Her hair was unkempt, her sky-blue wrapper haphazardly tied so that part of her breast and white undies were exposed. Her chubby body had gone. What was left was a skeletal entity. She was flicking her hands in the air as if she was dancing to Yahooze beat.

When my eyes caught hers, she called my name, became quiet and cuddled her legs, resting her chin on her knees. In her place now were a plate of pap and four balls of akara. The food was untouched. Perhaps the last food she was given before her escape.

My eyes swept across the entire room. It surprised me to see how neatly everything was arranged. No rippled bed, no clothes on the bed, no pairs of shoes kicked away in every corner. Perhaps Dad had asked our house helper, Nneoma, to clean up the mess. But why did she leave the food?

I needed something of Mum, something with her smell to hold onto, something that would bring her memory back to me. I opened her wardrobe. I took my time caressing each item of her clothing with tears raining down from my eyes.

In the middle of her clothing collection, my hand felt something thick. It was in her blue jeans, the ones I bought for her on the last Mothering Sunday we celebrated before she broke down. I put my hand on the pocket and pulled something out. It was a red jotter with a thick cover.

I opened it.

The leaves of the journal were all torn out but one. On the centre of the page she inscribed in bold letters:

12/4/2000

I SAW HIM TODAY.

Saw who? I turned the page. There was a drawing of a heart with an arrow piercing through it. Nothing more. Who did she see? C'mon, speak to me, Mum.

"Gozie… Gozie…" my dad called from the parlour. I put the jotter in the back pocket of my black trousers.

"I am coming."

*

Police. Two of them. They were in their early forties, judging from their physical appearances. One was in a uniform and the other wore navy blue trousers and a white long-sleeved shirt. The one in uniform sat on the sofa. The other sat at his left with a jotter in his hand. Dad was toying with his key, which had a small sticker on it with the inscription, ARSENAL FOR LIFE. The two cops were looking at me when I entered, but pretended that they were taking random glances just like you would do if you sat in a conference and in front of you was a charming young woman.

I greeted them.

"Take a seat," Dad said with a pulpit voice, waving to a seat on his right.

I went there and sat.

"These are the cops that will help us find your mum.

They were here yesterday when you weren't around and checked our property."

The one on the sofa cleared his throat and said, "I am Mat. We are from zone two, Uwani police station. Accept our sympathy and we assure you that we will do our best."

I nodded.

"I understand that you are her only child in Nigeria, the other is studying abroad?"

I nodded again.

"There are certain questions we need you to answer to aid our investigation. Are you ok with that?"

I nodded again.

They began their questions, which were centred on who were mother's friends or enemies and the last time such people had come in contact with her. Dad would interject at different occasions to show that he was the only true friend Mum had had. Before they left, they asked me to contact them if I suspected anything.

"Trust your instinct."

When they had gone, Dad told me that we would travel to see some of my maternal uncles in the evening.

"Why?" I asked.

"You can't predict these locals and how they reason. I have been hiding this from them. If they hear this from a secondary source, they may start thinking that I used your mother for some crazy ritual. You know most of them think backwardly."

*

I sneaked into the toilet. I was tired of Dad invading the privacy of my room, leaning on the wall, hands tucked in his trousers, with his 'I just came to check on you.' Perhaps this

10

was his means of reassuring me that everything remained the same. I posted a note on my door for him.

Gone to the toilet. Suffering from acute diarrhoea.

I brought out the diary from where I left it in my pocket. I sat at the white ceramic bowl of the toilet, pretending not to be bothered by the smell of camphor and antiseptic oozing out from it. I opened her journal. I read the inscription over and over again as if I were cramming it.

The first question that struck my mind was where was the rest of the journal? Clearly it was torn and the person that did it showed no pretence over it. It was haphazardly done. A lot of the edges of the torn leaves were still stuck in the jotter. Who did this and why did he leave only one leaf remaining?

A knock at the door. It was Dad.

"I am still here. The diarrhoea is terrible." I took a heavy breath as if I was battling with some faeces refusing to be let out.

"Then we have to go to a hospital."

"I am not going anywhere."

"Are you masturbating?"

Fuck you. I didn't say that.

*

"Sorry that you are passing through this," my dad said.

We were in his grey 406 Peugeot car going to my mother's home. He was driving. I sat beside him looking out through the window. I wound down the window to allow some air to flow in. I was allergic to the smell of disinfectant or air fresheners, but in front of me was a yellow Air Wick. I preferred sitting in the back but that wouldn't be possible with Dad. He had told our driver not to drive us so that he would have a private moment with me as we went. Although I knew I wasn't in the mood for discussing anything with anybody, with Dad I had no choice. In fact, it was one of those existential crosses I had to bear for being his son.

I didn't know what to say so I decided to cast my mind away from him by looking through the window, watching trees running past us. Starting from my childhood I had always thought that it was the car that was constant and the trees that sped by. My father had corrected me often then that it was the reverse. "Things most often aren't the way they are seen," he said. It is strange that, up till now, I still think the same way I thought over twenty years ago. When I got bored of watching those trees, I adjusted and returned my focus back to the car. My eyes met those of my father. The way he jerked nervously like a lad caught stealing fish from his mother's pot told me that perhaps he had been watching me for a long time.

His right hand reached my left hand where I rested it on my lap. His left hand on the steering wheel, his eyes rested mainly on me; he only stole a few glances watching out for an oncoming vehicle. He squeezed my hand tenderly.

"You have been the same always," he said.

"How?" I asked.

"Since you were a child, I have watched you whenever I was in the car with you. You often look through the window and whenever you do, it means that you have an enormous thing under your skin."

"I..."

"I really want you to share that with me."

I once again looked away through the window.

To start with, I never knew I had the character of being bothered with thought whenever I glance out the window.

Perhaps my father was right, because oftentimes, we are what we never knew we were, and it is that part of ourselves that we hardly change until a close person brings it to our knowledge. But even if this was truth, I think it was pretentious for Dad to claim ignorance of what was bothering me. Or did he just forget because it wasn't his cup of tea? Or was he seeking something else from me? The jotter; did he know about it?

"Things aren't this way, you know," he broke my thought. "Your mum was great. We had good times when we had you, Uche and Ebuka. That was when we bought our 504."

It became clearer to me now why Dad had banned Uche and me from using the white Peugeot car after Uche, my elder brother, had had an accident with it. That was four years ago when my mother's illness began. Dad had parked the car at an extreme end in our compound, which Onyinye had nicknamed 'extra-large compound,' and kept telling my mother then that it was a waste of a resource to have such massive land for a compound. Ever since then, it was only Dad who drove the car on a few occasions, but he would always be in it during the weekend taking a nap, head bent on the steering wheel. It amazed me that he didn't lock away the car's key in a safe somewhere in his room after his ban. He still kept it on the top of our 12-inch TV in the visitor's room. Perhaps it was still part of the memory he had with Mum, which he didn't want to lose hold of.

"She was an Arsenal fan too but then... but then…"

His voice sounded as if he was choking. I turned, and saw he was crying.

*

Uncle Odinaka was sitting at a white plastic seat under the shade of an udara tree near the trunk. He cupped his snuff on his right palm, and with his left, he tapped it to sniff. He would sneeze and some of the brownish droplets from it would spread on his white singlet. I called the colour of the singlet white because I knew when it had been that colour, when Mum bought it for him as a gift. What remained of it now was something yet to have a proper name of its own. Sometimes he would use the edge of the yellow wrapper that was tied across his waist to clean up his streaming nose.

Dad parked a stone's throw from the udara tree where Odinaka sat. As he turned the engine off, I knew what he would say. "Don't eat anything from anybody except the ones I approve and don't shake hands with any of them." I never knew at what point this ritual began, but what I could recall was that since Ebuka, my eldest brother, died, Dad suspected that my mother's uncles killed him and would always give me this instruction if I travelled to my mother's home with him.

We walked towards Uncle Odinaka. When he saw us coming, he stood up and started towards us. I realized why Mum used him as an adage whenever she felt that we weren't eating as we ought to. "Do you want to be like a single 'I' like your Uncle Odinaka?" she would say. And truly, Odinaka looked like an 'I' with a flat stomach and bottom. He looked like a strong Sahara wind could blow him away.

From his gestures, I knew that he wanted to hug Dad as he did Mum whenever I came with her, but Dad just smiled, standing away from him. Dad tucked his palms in the pockets of his white kaftan. Odinaka understood Dad's gesture, so he withdrew. But I went near him and hugged him just the way Mum used to do. I knew that if the eyes were a sword, Dad would have slain me. I tried as much as I could to avoid his eyes. It was then that I told Uncle Odinaka that I was tired and needed some rest. He gave me the key to his house. I thanked him. Without looking at my father, I left them still standing under the tree.

*

In the visitor's room I bolted the door behind me. My hand went to my trousers. I brought out the journal. Again I read the entry:

12/4/2000
I SAW HIM TODAY

I turned over the page to the heart pierced with an arrow. I tried to make any meaning of it. But the more I struggled with that, the more confused I became. I was like that for almost thirty minutes when it occurred to me — I began scraping out the white paper that veiled the thick cover of the jotter. I saw:

LOOKING FOR MORE, COURTING TROUBLE. TRY BED.

*

When I came out of the house, Dad was still under the udara tree. About fifteen other extended relatives sat with him in a circle. From where I stood in front of Odinaka's bungalow, I couldn't make out what the discussion was about. The way Nna, my mother's nephew, who looked like a scarecrow,

15

was speaking and was swinging his right hand up and down and sometimes pointing an accusing finger at my father showed me that whatever it was, it wasn't funny. Toochi, Odinaka's younger brother, sitting on Nna's left, would sometimes shake his head. Odinaka sat on Nna's right, using his two palms intermittently to give Nna a gesture of calming down.

I looked away. My eyes again found my mother's jotter from my pocket and examined what she wrote with the hope of discovering something more from it. Nothing was forthcoming. My eyes went back to the udara tree.

Virtually everybody there was standing up. I think my father was in the middle because I couldn't see him. Whatever led to the present situation I couldn't tell but I was certain that if nothing was done my father's safety was in danger. I walked over.

Immediately when they saw me the commotion began to calm. Chidi, Ejike, Mmadu and Ude, the elderly older cousins of my mother began going to their seats.

"You have a week to provide our daughter or you will face our wrath," Nna said as I approached them.

By the time I reached them, they were in a conspiracy of silence. I greeted them. They responded in unison, as if they had rehearsed it like little children in a nursery school. My father's hand reached mine, pulling me to him. We were heading to our car. I just managed to throw Odinaka's key to him.

*

I expected my father to burst out in anger as he used to do when boxed into a corner, but he didn't. We drove home in silence. Even though I had a feeling of what I thought went

16

wrong in the meeting, I needed to hear it first-hand from him, but he didn't speak. He was busy in his own world. The only word he shared with me was when we got home and were about to come out of the car. He told me, "Your mother was deep. She isn't what you saw and what you think you know."

I wanted to ask him what he meant, but he slammed the door and entered his room.

*

I stole the key to Mother's room from where Dad hung it on a wall in his room while he was in the toilet. Since we returned from my mother's house, I had been monitoring his movements. He had locked himself up, producing some shrill sounds of falling metal objects, and murmuring. All these, in a way I couldn't explain, produced an awkward feeling of fear inside me. When I heard his door open and I saw him rushing out, clutching his crotch, I immediately sneaked in.

Mum's room was dark. I leaned my back on the wall and waited for my father to be done with his business in the toilet before I began my searching, since a corridor linked my mother's room to the toilet and then to my father's. It turned out that he went for the complete cycle, as we jokingly called it among ourselves at school. When I heard the door of his room click, I turned on the light of my Nokia phone. I went to the edge of the wooden platform bed and began hunting. I started at the northern side where her head used to rest. I checked for an encryption but nothing was there. I searched at the other end of the bed, went under the bed, but nothing. Where was the trail?

I sat down to think. I couldn't hear Dad's searching noise

any longer. Instead I heard the croak-like sound of his snoring.

As I flashed the torch on the wall, it caught the mirror, and the light reflected back in my eyes and blinded me. It was like a flash, as swift as a shooting star — the face of my mother in the mirror, bloody tears in her eyes streaming down.

I wanted to scream but my power of speech was gone. My jaw was wide open, but no sound came out. In fact it wasn't only the power of my voice that went on holiday, my entire nervous system did, and what was left of me were frozen feet, paralysed hands, and an immobile head. But this, just as it began, vanished. My body began functioning again.

My instinct was to run out of the room – and I followed it. Halfway to the door, a voice within me, its urgency like the scream of a drowning child I saw years ago in Ofi River, persuaded me to do otherwise. I stopped. The voice urged me to go back to the bed and search again. I walked back with a tensed body and a mouth drained of saliva.

I searched the bed again. The result was the same. But the voice inside me made me further my search, all the way to the mattress. I used my hand to rub across the foam. My hand stumbled on something with the shape of a paper. When did it get there? I slipped my hand under the cover and fetched out the piece of paper.

I know you will reach here but the bad news is, once here it may be too late for you to go back. Your father is not what you think. He knows them. He is them. They ate my son; they will still eat all of you. Run fast if you can.

Was this written for me? Certainly it wasn't part of her diary. I read it over again trying to make meaning out of her thought. What did Mum take Dad for?

"Arrrrrrr…!" A scream from Dad jerked me out of my thoughts. The scream was continuous. I ran as fast as I could to his room. I turned on his light. I saw him kicking his legs on the bed where he lay, struggling like a person being suffocated. He was still asleep.

I went to him, shook him to wake him up. By then his bare body was drenched in sweat. He woke and hugged me like a kid would his mother as a last resort when threatened by a nightmare. I held him close to my body, his head on my shoulder, mine on his chin. He was breathing heavily.

"Calm down, Dad, calm down." That was the only thing I found myself saying.

Later, he recovered from the shock, and detangled himself from me.

"You have to leave this house," he said.

"Why, Dad? "

"Your mother is evil, her spirit torments here as I speak to you," he said. "I told you that she is deep. She is not what you think. Leave this house. The house is possessed with her demon."

I checked my wristwatch. It was 12 am.

"So you are telling me that she is dead?"

"She is not dead. She knows how to manipulate her spirit out of her body. That is Cherubim and Seraphim for you. That Church ruined her life."

"Why is she haunting us?"

"To get what she wants. But now I don't know what she needs. You see I don't want anything to happen to you. I will be still going in the morning to meet her relatives for the second time about her being missing. If anything happens to you, it will be my funeral, a kind of confirmation that I am the one responsible for her disappearance."

"Nothing will happen to me, Dad."

"I am not asking you to believe, I am telling you what to do. Leave this house."

"Where do you want me to go Dad? It is 12 am."

"Anywhere… anywhere."

He closed his eyes and lay back on the bed, cuddling his two legs. Deep within me I knew that I had to leave. That was how my father works. Comply with his dogmatic instruction first and come for negotiation later.

*

In the wardrobe I divided how I hung my clothes in two halves. On the left side of the wardrobe were my pairs of trousers, six of them. In the middle were my two baggy shorts. The other half of the wardrobe had at its extreme my jumpers and trainers, then there were my polo t-shirts and long and short sleeve shirts. My undies were piled in a white plastic bucket, resting on the base of the wardrobe.

My hands were akimbo as I was thinking on the clothes I needed. Deep within me, I knew that wherever I was going, I wasn't going to stay long.

I brought my school bag near the wardrobe. I collected ash jean trousers, a red t-shirt polo, a jumper and two undies. I went to my toilet, collected my red towel and sponge that I hung on the back of the door. At the edge of the sink was my herbal toothpaste and toothbrush, on the wall just above the sink was a mirror. I went there to collect the toothbrush and the paste. I slightly raised my head to the mirror. I saw something like a human shadow, difficult to differentiate whether it belonged to a man or a woman, pass in a twinkle of an eye. Coldness descended on my body. I waited. I looked again, but saw nothing.

*

"Bullshit," I murmured as I slammed my hands on the steering wheel of my car. I was in my deep blue Mercedes 190, trying for ages to start it. It was as if my car battery was dead. No matter how I tried to turn the ignition, the car never responded.

I thought what to do next. To use my mother's Honda Jeep? I declined the idea. If she wanted to get at me as my father had said, I had this feeling that it would be easier for her in her car. Dad's 406 Peugeot wasn't an option either. That would anger him and arm him with more reasons why he would maintain his stand on the exile he was sending me to. The only option left was the white 504 Peugeot.

I entered the house and collected the car key. Next, I was heading to my school hostel, Zik, at the University of Nigeria, Nsukka, to pass the night.

*

There was a buzzing, vibrating under my pillow and shaking my head. I felt like I was in a dream, and I was conscious of the dream in another dream. It stopped but came again and threw a spanner into the wheels of my much-needed rest. I lifted the heavy weight of sleep from my tired brows and lifted my pillow. It was my phone that was vibrating. Dad was calling.

I picked up the call, yawning and stretching my body, still lying on my bed. My head was hammered and peppered by a headache and I felt it spinning.

"You took the 504. Are you crazy?" he screamed. "What happened to your car?"

"Dad..."

21

"Don't Dad me. Bring that car home immediately."
He cut the phone.

*

Outside, I watched our school garden that was converted to a hanging zone. The hanging zone was in the middle of Zik's and Belewa hostel. The two hostels were opposite each other but were linked by a hallway. There the dry, hot, and dusty wind of harmattan was tossing dried leaves, pieces of paper, clothes, and sand around. Sometimes it spanned the rubbish in a circular form, tall like a pole and moving in a fast velocity like the torrent of a river. Twenty years ago, Uche would threaten me that he would drag me to the cyclone whose destination was the land of women with half skeletal body and the other part flesh, and they would marry me off to their princess or make me their pet. I would cuddle Mum who would assure me that Uche's words were mere vain threat.

A male student in ripped grey tracksuit trousers was battling with the harmattan cyclone in the hanging zone over his clothes that swayed around. He dove, rescuing an olive green sweatshirt, but he wasn't lucky with his two white boxers. He cursed and watched the wind take the boxers and drop them on the top of the zinc of Belewa's hostel.

Apart from him, the whole school was deserted like a graveyard. The twit-twooing of owls made me shiver with fear. I came to where I had parked my car in a space in the front of the Zik's hostel; the back left tyre of my car had gone flat.

"Holy shit," slipped from my mouth unconsciously.

I had no option but to change the tyre and drive the car back home before Dad descended on me with his mad rage.

I opened the trunk with the hope of finding a spare tyre. There were two red candles tied together with a tattered piece of a red cloth, a red paperback titled *Evening Worship of the Sons' of Light* with my father's name written across its spine in red ink, and then the tyre I was looking for.

When had Dad been religious?

A feeling came to me to search my father's room. It occurred to me that he would be going to my mother's home as he told me before I left the house last night. If I had to search, it would be when he would be meeting my mother's uncles.

I called Father to tell him about the flat tyre. I lied, telling him that the car engine was having problems too. I wanted to use the time I would buy with the lie to keep him away from worrying me to come home quick so that I could figure out how to break into his room.

"Come back before evening, in fact before I return from my in-laws," he yelled. "I need the car then. Drop it and leave the house. I don't want to meet you at home when I come back. You have terribly annoyed me. "

*

Dad's door opened after I had loosened the bolts of the lock with my screw. Ejiofor, my friend who is a carpenter, had given me the suggestion.

"Act fast and fix the lock back," he admonished.

Inside Dad's room, I was surprise to see the bed dressed in a red bed sheet with two red pillowcases. At the middle of the bed was a wooden red cross. He had changed the purple curtains that were in the room even as of yesterday to red plain ones. A surreal feeling engulfed me. The saliva in my mouth drained away.

My mind told me to check over the wardrobe. It was locked. I had to loosen it just as I did to the door. No clothes were in it. In place of them was a wooden red table three inches high. A red table cloth covered it. Two red candles were standing on a red candle stand. A book, *Rite of Sacrifice,* was opened and faced downwards on the altar.

Cold from nowhere descended upon me. My mouth was shaking, body trembling. I picked up the book. At the top of the page, in a bold print was:

INSTRUCTION: ON THE WEEK OF SACRIFICE, NO ONE MEMBER OF THE BROTHERHOOD WOULD BE ON THE PREMISE WHERE THE SACRIFICIAL LAMB WOULD BE CONSUMED.*

My eyes scan the entire page. At its bottom, in a fine print was:

* TO DISOBEY THE ABOVE INSTRUCTION, THE VICTIM WOULD BE BLESSED WITH MENTAL ILLNESS OR INCURABLE DISEASE.

The book slipped from my hands unconsciously and fell on the ground.

I heard a sound of metal falling on the ground, something like a cup or a plate. My heart skipped a beat. I listened, nothing came forth. I started having a strange feeling that Dad may be on his way.

I rushed out of our house. As I did, a lot of thoughts were on my mind. I wondered whether Mum had witnessed Ebuka's sacrifice and she had been blessed with madness? Whether the haunting spirit I had experienced came from Dad's cult and Dad had been faking being haunted too in order to get rid of me? And I thought of what Mum had written in the rest of her journal, and where had the journal gone? Tears were streaming down my eyes. As I walked away from the house confused on what next to do, I knew that I was not going to set my foot in it again in my life. I knew that I wouldn't be courageous enough to confront my father. I would call Uche and tell him what I saw. I would also do the same with Uncle Odinaka, hoping that he would sort whatever out. I would break my phone SIM card, and delete my Facebook and Twitter accounts. Change my name. I would try to find another life elsewhere, hoping that this nightmare would not haunt me forever.

THE LAST MAN STANDING

When the government announced their ban on what they termed 'non-essential foodstuffs', I didn't fully understand the implication until two weeks later, when I went to buy a Sprite, a drink I was addicted to. My father had been, too. When he was still alive I remember people calling him 'Mr. Sprite'. If you were near, he would shake hands with a smile. With children, he stroked their hair. When he was in a hurry or a distance apart, he waved. He only rushed when he was going to the coal mine at Coal Camp, Enugu, the site that had first attracted white men to Enugu City. They had then established their house at New Heaven, leaving peasant workers in Coal Camp. My father had preferred living in Abakpa, a town on the outskirts of Enugu City, with a lot of indigenes of our own tribe, but this was where he could find work. That was before independence.

At the store, they said Sprite was not in stock. Not in stock? That was silly.

I was still battling to comprehend this when they made subsequent bans. Numerous food items were added to the list. Indo-mie, Spaghetti, Macromie, Bobo, Biscuit, all were given their final funeral rites. The Minister of Information said that we were in a state of emergency, fighting ADAIDS. The production of those banned foodstuffs was a waste of manpower and would not help the majority of the citizens suffering from the epidemic.

Advanced Acquired Immune Deficiency Syndrome (ADAIDS) had a long, complicated history. Rumour had it that a couple of scientists from Germany and America were sponsored by UNICEF to conduct a genetic experiment, using an AIDS virus. The experiment allegedly took place in the Sahara Desert, near the northern part of Nigeria, in an underground lab. Nobody has ever given a correct description of the place. Most people believed it was destroyed immediately after the experiment failed. The experiment, aimed at producing a cure for AIDS, instead ended up producing a mutated type of AIDS that could be contracted from sexual intercourse, even when one was wearing a condom. Worse, the disease remained dormant until three months before death, making it easier to spread. Once someone contracted it, the person never lived beyond three years. After the experiment was shown to be a failure, UNICEF came in and silenced all who needed to be silenced.

Some said that all those who had anything to do with the experiment were assassinated. Others believed they were heavily bribed.

I do not know if this is true.

The most popular story of the origin of the disease was that some Fulani nomadic cattle herders in northern Nigeria, victims of HIV, had intercourse with their cows. The HIV virus in their bodies reacted with another virus in the cow's body and it resulted in a mutated AIDS. The ADAIDS was transmitted to Igbo prostitutes in the southern part of the country (the tribal people used to believe they could literally march through hellfire if money were discovered in the Devil's hand) by those nomadic cattle herders, and to their women when they went home. With time, thanks to sex, as a fire that catches a cluster of palm thatch roofing spreads, the disease spread everywhere.

To worsen matters, the government stretched out its hand to non-food stuffs. We were constrained to watch only one local TV station and also to listen to one radio station.

Two of my favourite programs, *Hyper Fear* and *Dance like the Dead*, were struck off and their producers reassigned. They gave us the same reason: 'lack of manpower'.

One amusement park was permitted in each state and a maximum of three secondary schools. All the universities were reduced to one, with only two faculties: Medical Sciences and Engineering. They believed that the medical academics were the only relevant faculty that could handle the plague of ADAIDS. As for Engineering, they kept the infrastructure from breaking down. So, we still had electricity. For the rest: 'a waste of manpower'.

I found out from afternoon broadcasts of the BBC and Radio Nigeria that the UN had abolished the flow of aid workers to the country. Soon I ceased to hear any further pronouncements made by the government. One day, like a joke, the government was dead! Gone. No more announcements, no nothing. It dawned on me that, with the death of the government, other things, like electricity, would follow suit.

I decided to place an announcement at Radio Nigeria, the only surviving station and the first to be established immediately after independence.

The announcement would invite everybody living in Enugu City to come and live in Uwani Town, to fight loneliness with 'African communalism', since the disease was winning every other battle. I was sure not all of us had contracted the disease. I hadn't.

I was not at risk. My illiterate mother had not taken prenatal vitamins during her pregnancy. So I had contracted a disease in youth that had rendered me a eunuch. But I had hopes that married couples who were faithful to each other and children would also survive.

At first, I was optimistic. I walked out of my bungalow,

where I lived alone on Nnaji Street in Uwani. The street was empty. One could hardly recognise the black colour of the road tar. Mud had painted it red.

I walked to the major road, where I could get a bus-taxi that would take me to the station. For hours, I stood waiting. No taxi came. A Peugeot pickup drove past me. The back was loaded with a corpse. Two young men were sitting in the front with the driver. I didn't need any person to tell me where they were going. I had done a similar thing in my street many times.

The corpse was going to be disposed of in a big pit dug at the outskirts of town. They would then incinerate it. It eventually became clear to me that taxis had died a natural death, just like our government. I decided to go back home and use my car. I still had gas.

When I got to the radio station, I was lucky to see the studio manager, Mr. Dudu, standing, arms akimbo, in front of the building. A man as short as Zacchaeus. God forgive me; I hope that is not a cliché. We shook hands.

I told him of my mission. He accepted, but quickly informed me he had just broadcast an announcement: The disease had developed a more virulent strain. Any person who remained with a victim of the disease in an enclosed area for about two hours would also become infected. He said that a Professor Dimbo Theresa from the University of Nigeria had brought him these findings and asked him to air them. The manager then warned me of the dangers of gathering a large crowd of people with my intended announcement.

I considered his warning. There were few of us left in Uwani and plenty of houses for the remaining people, if the mortality rate here had been the same as in other Enugu towns. I was sure there wouldn't be any risk of transmission.

30

He agreed, and my announcement was a success. People turned out, though few in number. To my surprise, Professor Dimbo Theresa was among those who came to join us.

The few of us who remained eagerly waited, listening to the news to hear which new government would seize power, but none came. We were still waiting when the last surviving radio and TV stations vanished. The first day I turned on my radio and was confronted by the reality that the station was no longer working, it seemed to me like a doomsday. But weeks later, we had all become accustomed to the new reality.

As time went on, and people died out, I had to drive my car from where I was living in Uwani to New Heaven, Abakpa and Emene to see if anyone was still there. I usually did that with an old Peugeot pick-up. The reason was to avoid disease transmission. If I saw anybody, that person would have to stay in the open, in the back, during the journey.

But apart from the few of us who were still living in Uwani, I found no other human life in the other cities. I decided to expand my search. I moved from Enugu City to nearby towns. I headed towards faraway Ninth-Mile, at the other end of Enugu State. Dominated purely by Igbo tribes, the indigenes there had been converted to Christianity, like those who had lived in Enugu. The difference was that, in other towns in Enugu, apart from Abakpa, there were also non-Igbo tribes and Muslims.

I stopped along the way to fill my tank. When I reached a filling station, it was deserted. I remembered, just a few years ago, how boisterous the place had been. I could still recall how I had manoeuvred to get my tank filled first, especially during times of fuel scarcity. Such actions usually elicited howling and shouting from other drivers. I lusted for those times now.

There was no attendant to refill my tank. It occurred to me that, if the fuel was exhausted, there was no one to ask for more. There was also no electricity and I soon found I couldn't refill my tank. I looked around, hoping for a lucky break.

Some parts of the roof of the filling station had been blown down by wind. The white paint of the walls had been washed by the rain. Green lichen had started to grow on the side of the building.

I went into the building and pushed a door open.

I was surprised that the door wasn't locked. I had been thinking I would have to break it down. Under the dust and cobwebs, the pink paint on the wall remained intact. I guessed that it was the manager's office, because, sitting with his head bent on a table, was the decaying, stinking corpse of a man.

Beside his head were bundles of money. "Igbo and money, just like bread and butter!" I murmured, as I quickly closed the door.

The next door was locked and I had to search for the key in the manager's pocket, holding my breath. Inside a small room sat the station's generator.

Thank God it functioned, as did the fuel pump — a miracle. I got my tank filled and drove off. The road was lonely. Not a surprise. I knew it would demand another miracle for another car to drive by. If that ever happened, I would celebrate.

When I reached Ninth-Mile, I had to slow down, peeping through the windshield. No one was in sight. I then took a path that led to the heart of the town and parked at a village health centre, a house with green walls. In the old days, the place would have been crowded with people waiting for a doctor. By now, tall, elegant grasses were already overtaking the area.

I left the building and followed another path. The only sounds in the town were the cries of wild animals: monkeys and, sometimes, hyenas and carrion birds like the kite and the owl.

The path brought me to a primary school. Beside it stood a market already in ruins. The shops seemed like anthills of the savannah, telling the new grasses about last year's bush burning. I entered the school building, painted yellow outside and white inside, and moved from one classroom to another, praying for luck. Each door I opened, I either saw lizards playing or rats making love.

I looked at a board in the last classroom. Despite water damage, 'Class Five' could still be read, although faintly.

There was a noise. If I hadn't been fast, I wouldn't have seen it. A long, coiled black snake, at least four feet long, nested among the empty desks. It raised its head. Its neck was dim white with black stripes. A cobra. The type our villagers called 'Tomorrow is far', because you would not live to see the next day once bitten by it. It seemed to say: Who is this man who is treading on my territory? Before I could leave the room, it came at me.

I backed away quickly, unsure if it was attacking or defending. It recoiled itself and sprang, throwing itself at me. I managed to dodge and it missed its target.

I saw a broom lying nearby. I picked it up.

The snake sprang erect, spat its venom. But I was far from it, so all the saliva poured on the ground.

It was now my turn to attack. With my stick, I reached for it. It then recoiled itself and threw itself on me another time. I dodged again. It landed on the ground and my stick was on it. I never gave it a chance. I kept on striking till it was dead.

Then I walked away, sweating. I was breathing heavily and I was sure my blood pressure was high.

I wanted to go home.

I ran through the town, shouting, asking for someone to come out. I found myself on the path again. Part of me kept telling me to just get in my car and drive back home. The other part insisted I continue with the search. Perhaps someone remained in the village. I listened to that part.

I went through the village. Most of the buildings were intact, though with peeling paint. At every house, I shouted, "Is anybody there?" Getting no result, I moved on. I hoped that, if anyone survived, they would answer me. However, due to the encounter with the snake, I was afraid of entering any house.

I gave up. On my way back to my car, I heard a voice.

A child stood in a doorway, a girl of about thirteen. I ran to her and held her tight. I was overwhelmed with joy. A joy that knew no bounds. She was weak and looked famished. She began to weep. I consoled her and took her to the car, where I kept her at the back.

Back home, we had a celebration as never before. One of us, I can't remember who, said that this was a sign that God had not abandoned humanity yet.

But amidst the celebration, some were sceptical of her. They wondered how a little girl could be the only survivor in her village. What did she have that others didn't?

Rumours began, the most popular being that she was a witch. I think Mrs. Chioma, a woman living across the street, originated this version of the story.

Mrs. Chioma claimed to be a witch doctor. According to her, she never knew that she had the gift until a crisis rocked her family. It began when she gave birth to her fourth child. She had employed a nanny to help her look after her baby, so that she could still meet the demands of her housework. But, unknown to her, the nanny was a blood-tasting witch.

A few months after the nanny arrived, Mrs. Chioma's children got sick.

Her first child died. She was still recovering from this shock when the second one also died, just six months later. As if that were not enough, the two children left were critically ill. None of the seven hospitals they were taken to could diagnose the problem.

Then a friend advised her to try a native doctor. The native doctor told her that she had the power to heal herself and her children, and that he could help her learn how. He gave her some herbs, which she was to boil and mix in her meals. Three days later her inner eyes opened. She then saw how her children's nanny turned into a big mosquito at night to suck her children's blood, which she would, in turn, transmit to other witches in their nightly meetings as their meal. She had to exorcise the nanny before sending her packing. She had since lost her husband and her remaining children to the disease.

I heard Mrs. Chioma, more than once, telling people that the little girl had a big tooth on her forehead. She even said it was the girl who killed her parents, not the disease.

I asked her, if the little girl was truly the cause of her parents' death, what of the rest in the village? Was she also responsible for that?

She retorted, "The girl helped the disease in escalating the death rate in their village." According to her, when the girl saw what the disease was doing, she availed herself of that opportunity and started sucking blood as much as she could.

If people had only seen her as a gossip among those of us who were living on Nnaji Street, I wouldn't have considered it a problem. The problem was that she instigated people.

At first it began with people being afraid of the girl. From that, it escalated to direct verbal abuse. I can't now precisely remember the person, but I can still recall hearing somebody, one day, exclaiming to her that she was a witch who had come to kill us all, as she did her own people. The peak of the whole thing came when an angry mob stormed my bungalow. They needed to exorcise her. Unsurprisingly, the mob leader was Mrs. Chioma.

I refused to yield to their demand. But they threatened that if I didn't release the girl, they would certainly catch her.

As this was by no means an empty threat, not only was she now living in my bungalow, I took her with me wherever I went. The accusations never stopped. On the contrary, they got worse! Whenever anyone died, she was the cause. As each day went the pressure of her potential exorcists increased.

I would have yielded to their demand were it not for the timely intervention of Professor Dimbo Theresa.

Professor Dimbo offered to carry out a test on the girl. She saw the case in another light. For her it was a step towards finding a cure to the disease, if one could actually find out what made the girl different from the rest of her village.

And, although she was fiercely warned that this was a case beyond science, Professor Dimbo was not one who would easily go back on her decision.

Within a week after this test, Mrs. Chioma, herself, died. With their worst instigator gone, the mob faded and the pressures on me subsided. Professor Dimbo later revealed her findings. It was as startling as it was ordinary: The little girl had sickle cell anaemia. Anybody blessed with this ailment has a greater resistance to the ADAIDS — similar to the immunity they had to malaria.

In the subsequent days, I went on more searches. None yielded results.

After a month, I became tired and abandoned the project.

The survivors in Uwani dwindled.

They all died.

I became worried for the girl, because she was still so sickly, and hoped I would die first, but it was not to be. She died yesterday.

I have burned my dead. My suitcase is in the car; my supplies are packed.

I carry with me the knowledge of the sickle cell anaemia, and hope this may be of use some day.

I am heading to no destination in particular.

One day, I will find another living human.

But for now, I am the last man standing.

EXORCISM

I knew it was 'him' because people who had unfinished business with him during the day would come to me at night and call me Ifeanyi. Like the grey eyed woman with the Ghana hair weave, plump checks, and the breasts that I knew wouldn't fit in any generic bra. Even in her customized ones, the breasts would still be peeping out. I nicknamed her *One Day One Trouble* because every night she would come to me with a complaint. Yesterday it was a computer. She said, "Ifeanyi, did you fix that computer for me?"

Fuck you and Ifeanyi, I didn't say; I yawned as if I were tired and told her, "Sorry I forgot. Would you mind coming tomorrow morning?" I knew by then, it was Ifeanyi's turn to own our body and, damn with him, he could sort the issue out.

Over the years, I had discovered that it was more convenient for me to take responsibility for the irresponsible actions of my body-mate. The incident that made me take the decision was when one athletic built guy, who could easily fit in as a cocaine baron I had watched in a Hollywood movie, demanded a memory stick he had asked Ifeanyi to buy for him. I was pissed off. I told him, "Fuck off." What I saw again was that punch that kept my nose bleeding throughout the night. That guy had a lot of anger, or perhaps Ifeanyi had annoyed him too much.

Ifeanyi had a talent at angering people, judging from the numerous numbers of people who came at night with one complaint or the other, especially about computer stuff and other related matters. And the damned horse hardly got a job done. Not only that, his attitude towards our body made me feel like strangling him, had we the opportunity of seeing ourselves. Every night, when I became aware of my existence, I would be suffering from one physical pain or the other. Yesterday it was a cut at my wrist. Day before yesterday, it was a stab through my palm. In short, this week was hand's week; all injuries were inflicted there. Who knew what part of our body he would reach next week?

My desire to talk to him had made me to try at different occasions to hang on, to survive or to escape that moment at which I would feel my heart pounding heavily on my ribs and a cold breeze would move through my legs, caressing as it went through my spine to my head. Once on my head, I would be knocked off. When I would again know that I existed would be around 8 pm of the next day. It happened in a blink of an eye. If it wasn't for the wall clock that hung in my bedroom, I would assume a second had come and gone.

Yesterday, in my attempt to talk to him, I wrote this on a piece of paper for him:

I know you are called Ifeanyi because your customers come at night and call me your name. I answer it for lack of name and more for the fact that I don't want people to feel strange about one person who insists in answering two different names at different times of the day. That tells you who I am. That I am gentle and co-operative person. Now that we have found ourselves stuck together in a single boat, I think we need to know ourselves more. Can you tell me who you are?

I didn't just want to tell him to stop that cutting of our body or to be nice to people. I wanted to gain his trust. That is common sense. If we achieved this, we could easily proceed to other things.

I kept the letter at the edge of our bed precisely at the top of his yellow *Good News Bible*. I then used his prayer bead to hold it. I guessed that that was likely the first place he would go when he took over our body. It was the only place in our room he kept neat. Each night, my first work was to re-arrange the shoes he'd kicked into every corner of the house, clothes on the bed, bed unmade. In anger, I would tear the bible quotes he copied and pasted on the wall. But before getting rid of them, I would read them. 'Rescues me lord… the lord is my shepherd… into your hands I commend my spirit…'. And he ended each with an initial 'C' at the right side of the bottom of the piece of paper.

He didn't put any reply back at the bible. I felt that he put it where he thought I often go in the house. I began my search around the room. I went to the bathroom. I knew he must know I was the one washing our body for us. This reminded me of something else. Each night I inherited the body there was this rancid smell emitting from our private parts. I think he used to rub something there, but his aim of doing that I couldn't fathom.

The reply wasn't in the bathroom.

I searched around the parlour, came back to the bedroom, and ripped away the white bed sheet and the two pillow cases, no nothing. I went to the wardrobe, searched our clothes one after the other. Our clothes were all in a black colour. I had attempted to introduce varieties of other colours to our wardrobe by buying cheap pink shirts and blue jean trousers at the street market that thrives at night in our street, Nnaji Street, Enugu. But he never allowed them to stay till the next day. Where those clothes ended I never knew. What I could tell was that the following day after I

41

bought it, it would be missing from the wardrobe. I had the urge to take some of the black trousers and burn them, but I didn't because as the slogan said 'if a madman takes your clothes while you are having a bath and you chase him naked, you are mad too.' Aside from that, he was the day dweller, the one that needed the clothes most. I hardly go anywhere.

In the wardrobe there was nothing.

By this time my stomach began rumbling, some of the worms in my stomach were fighting and others were somersaulting because of the lack of food. I abandoned the search and went down to the kitchen. At the kitchen I went to our medium fridge with a sticker of Jesus crowned with thorns with blood splashed on his forehead. Ifeanyi had a lot of agonizing Christs pictures around the house, with Jesus Christ written underneath as if to say that Christ was missing and his parents or one of his beloved apostles had gone to a police station and reported the case. The police in turned had made copies of the picture of the missing Jesus with his name written underneath with the promise of a ransom to anyone with useful information.

I hoped that there would be food in the fridge because I left some there last night. Anyway, Ifeanyi had a knack of eating up any remaining food I left. One day I was walking across our street and noticed a restaurant with an inscription, 'don't cook, just eat.' I thought that that would be an appropriate synonym for Ifeanyi's name.

I opened the fridge.

My food was gone, not a surprise. But the surprise was that in place of it was a piece of paper soaked in water. What was Ifeanyi trying to say, that I was a food addict? That was perhaps why out of everywhere in the house he chose to keep his reply on the fridge. Think of it, I was the one that only ate once in a day, just my supper, but Ifeanyi takes breakfast and lunch.

But that wasn't my headache. What I needed now was to know what he thought of me and the conversation that would start from it. I brought out the letter. The blue ink used in writing it had already been soaked in water that came from somewhere in the fridge making it blurred for me to read anything from it. Miraculously, the greeting, 'Dear Chioma' was still faintly seen.

Wait. Did he think that I was a woman?

A knock interrupted my thought. Here we go. Another complaint.

I shuffled to the parlour. When I opened the door, it was *One Day One Trouble*. "Hello," I said.

"Can I come in?" she asked and she didn't even permit me to finish locking the door properly before she was on me, kissing. I pulled her away from myself, managing to give her a smile.

She said, "I don't know what is wrong with you."

"I am sorry. You know, I love you but I am weak."

She shrugged her shoulders and walked past me, swinging her hip and twisting her bottom in her white mini skirt. I could see the semi-circle curve of her bottom, how each half came together and joined in an interlocking kiss. I knew that she wanted me to see this; if not, why did she come without undies?

She sat on my sofa.

"Why are you there like a statue? You said you were tired, you can't even sit down. I have something to talk over with you," she said.

In my mind I told her to walk off, hit the road but in reality I walked to the sofa opposite where she sat and dumbed myself.

43

"What is that you need to discuss with me?"

I was not looking at her when I was asking this question, my eyes were rather on her legs. Her mini skirt barely covered her chocolate laps and she constantly acted as if she was forcing the skirt to do the work, which in all righteousness it was never meant to do.

I avoided my eyes moving upward even though I knew that her legs were in such a way that my eyes could see her central bank had I wished to. For the first time since I knew her, I began noticing that my hand was trembling as if I was suffering from Parkinson disease, and my mouth was drained of saliva.

"What did you want to discuss with me?" I repeated. Now I wasn't sure whether I pronounced every word of it right.

She stood up. My eyes met hers. She winked and there was something in her eyes that I couldn't forge a name for but I think it was of someone having a passion burning inside. She began walking towards me while licking her tongue.

Was she the Chioma?

"Chioma stop this drama," I said.

"Chioma? Who is Chioma? Your madness have not stopped? So it has come to the extent that you can't differentiate me from Chioma, eh?"

She came closer, few inches away from where I sat, her body leaning on me. I adjusted, but her body kept coming closer, her breast was pressing on my face.

I wanted to push her away, but her words arrested me.

"Listen, babe," she said with a soothing voice like a lullaby mothers use to draw their children to sleep, "Chioma is of no use to you. She has never cared, did she? She broke your heart many times, abandoned you countless times.

Besides, she is dead."

"She is still alive," I said, trying to push the discussion further.

"So you stupidly think. Grow up man. The world is moving. Better tell yourself the bitter truth, she died in that fire accident. She was burnt, charred like a piece of paper."

"You are a liar."

"I am sure of that. Didn't you watch the whole thing on the TV? She was among the unidentified victims. Her body has rotted away by now in Kirikiri mass grave the government buried all of them. And you know what? Maggots are having their field day, marching through her mouth, to her skull and coming out through her eyes like soldiers in a parade."

Even though I wanted more information from her I couldn't withstand how she celebrated such news. I never knew when I pushed her away. She fell on the sofa beside me.

"Don't put your guilt on me. Had you bought the meat she asked you of, she wouldn't have gone to do the shopping?"

"Hold it there."

"Okay… ooo… but I will keep telling you the truth. Move on guy, the world is moving."

I left her in the parlour and ran upstairs, my feet sounding *bom… bom… bom* on the wooden stairs.

"Bitch… bitch…" I heard her shouting downstairs, slapping her palm on my sofa and smashing her legs on the ground.

I closed the door behind me and held the handle of my door, my head leaning on it.

"Bitch… bitch…" Her voice rang out. "You know it will not be long, you will forget this your Chioma and you will remember me. You will soon kneel down and beg me for what you are rejecting."

I remained where I was, my hand was trembling. Later I heard her sigh, and her loud shuffling as she walked out of the house. She banged the door behind her. I waited for about three minutes to make sure that she had long gone before I stepped out of my room and walked down to the parlour.

In the parlour, I sank on my seat. What kind of person was my body-mate?

I decided to search around the house to know whether I could stumble upon anything he had written to Chioma.

I went up again to the bedroom. On the top of the wardrobe he had a grey aluminium box. For long I had been procrastinating over my plan to search that box. I brought a wooden stool, which he kept in front of his reading table. I climbed on top of it. When I tried to access the bag, it was locked. I wanted to carry it down, but it was heavy. I pushed it down. It crashed with a sound of *kidim* on the ground, with its top breaking freely, and piles of papers and five books flew out and scattered on the floor.

I came down. The first book I picked was a white paperback with the title, *On Being a Stigma* by Abbot Henry Lewis. The second was also by the same author, with the title the *Stigma of Padre Pio*. The third and the fourth one was by him also. The only exception was the fifth book which had a brown hardcover, written by Savj Mondin, with the title, *On Cajoling the Spirit*. I leaned it against the wall beside me, making a mental note that I would read it later. The rest of the books I shoved back in the box.

I began picking the papers, scanning through all of them to see if I could stumble upon anything of interest. I was surprised to see that he had kept most of his writing in encrypting form. The ones he wrote in English language were the names of some people.

I was going through this, thinking of what it meant before I was interrupted by lightning that was followed by thunder. The sky opened its mouth and water flowed from it. Sometimes the rainfall splashed on my window, making it translucent. I watched the rain for a while and resumed my search. But a knock in the parlour interrupted me again. I hoped it was not *One Day One Trouble*. Did she forget anything here? I walked down to the parlour and opened the door. A man wearing soutane, clutching a black bible on his breast, was shivering at the door.

"Ifeanyi," he called.

I stepped aside. He entered. His face looked familiar. I remembered I saw him in a souvenir card at Ifeanyi's bible which had the title 'Kindly Pray for Fr. Ebuka on His Ordination.' His moustache looked like that of a cowboy in an American movie. I rent a lot of movies, but Ifeanyi doesn't keep them for me to watch. He returned them and brought in the place of them a video of Christ's crucifixion. Ifeanyi was a junkie to the movie. I knew by now he would memorize every bit of it.

I didn't know the correct way to approach this visitor. But he seemed to know the terrain of the house by the way he moved towards the red sofa in the parlour. Perhaps an intimate friend of Ifeanyi? I followed him closely.

He said, "Ifeanyi, did you pray that psalm?"

"I will do it in the morning," I replied.

"You are not Ifeanyi."

The way he said it showed me that he knew. But I wouldn't give in. I couldn't sell myself out.

"I am Ifeanyi."

He said, "Then tell me the psalm."

The game was up. It was then he began to pray: "*In nomen pater et filio et spiritus sanctus.* In the Name of Jesus Christ, our God and Lord strengthened by the intercession of the Immaculate Virgin Mary, Mother of God, of Blessed Michael the Archangel, of the Blessed Apostles Peter and Paul and all the Saints. And powerful in the holy authority of our ministry, we confidently undertake to repulse the attacks and deceits of the devil and to cast out the demon in the body of your humble servant…"

I tried to cut him short, to tell him that I wasn't the one that was tormenting and damaging the body. It was Ifeanyi who used whatever to cut it and rub the penis with a strange liquid. It was him who was in a traumatic relationship. I was the perfect guy. But the priest wouldn't listen. He continued, hoping to exorcize me.

HAUNTED GRAVE

"Ekene was alone in the abandoned cemetery," Chidi said, "on the top of a mango tree plucking the fruits when he noticed some smoke coming towards him. His eyes darted immediately following the smokes to its source. He saw that it was emanating from a grave yielding to the pull of a force shaking the ground as if the land was under the attack of an earthquake."

Up till now, I hadn't figured out why Chidi chose to be telling us a ghost story. Three of us, Obi, Chidi and I were in a graveyard chilling. The burial ground was near our school and it was where we often escaped boring teachers and extramural classes. Today it was Physics extramural tutorial. We had sneaked out of the classroom, pretending to go to a restroom when we saw the lanky Physics teacher who looked like a scarecrow in his oversize grey coat coming to teach. Our escape through the toilet was more convenient because the restroom was built separately from the rest of the school blocks. Notwithstanding that, the toilet wall still had the same painting with the rest of the school: pink up to the window level, and the remaining was with a white oil colour. Behind the toilet was a cluster of plantain trees. The ground was humid with an age long, accumulated decay of fallen plantain trunks and leaves. The stench oozing out of it was suffocating and pungent to the nose. Heat radiated out of the humid soil too. The standing stems of the plantain trees were nearer to each other, covering the whole ground up to the school fence, which was made of barbed wire. The shade of those plantain plants provided a perfect environment for sneaking out of the school by climbing through the fence, unknown to any prying eye and safe from the punishment of the school authority who often sanctioned offenders with one-week manual labour as a punishment for such an act. Once out of the fence, we would wait for each other patiently before strolling leisurely through a tiny route surrounded by spear grasses and elephant grasses, to the abandoned graveyard to dot away our time.

"Ekene was scared, goose bumps all over his body," Chidi continued as he picked a pimple on his left cheek, squeezing it. "He watched the dark smoke and the cracking tomb. The smoke was hitting his face, blurring his view, but he still managed to see what was going on. Not long, a hand with patches of rotten flesh that was paling away shot out from a tomb. The hand stretched out in the air, twisting its fingers one after the other."

The way Chidi jabbed his left hand into the air and began twisting it dramatically as if he was the dead rising from the tomb, startled Obi as well as myself. Obi had jerked back. The stick of the cigarette in his mouth fell down, bounced on his white shirt, and gave it an ash stain, but he managed to shift his left leg quickly and avoided the cigarette leaving its trail of ashes on his pink trousers too. The stick fell beside his leg, right in the front of me where I sat at the edge of a tombstone of one Ekene Okoro (1970-1985). That was all for his epitaph. I guessed that his relatives were too vexed for his early death that they cared not to leave any message of good wishes to him.

Obi reached for the fallen stick but my feet got at it first. I stamped at it.

"What the hell is wrong with you?" Obi asked me as he smacked his lips, frowning his face and rubbing his palm on his low trimmed haircut. Obi stole a look with the corner of his eyes at Chidi. Chidi was watching us, his left hand was playing with the sparely beard on his chin and his right hand was pressing the muscle of his left hand. The fruit of gym, he often called his muscle. Even though Chidi was the youngest among us at 17, (Obi was 21 and I, 19) he had this aura that he served as a ringleader among us. His gangster afro hair-style and muscular figure I think gave him this advantage.

"Your hygiene first," I wanted to tell Obi but I didn't. I found it so annoying to be giving the same explanation over and over again to an adult like Obi to stop picking his fallen consumable items back and eating. I wasn't afraid of him anyway, had he chosen to pick a fight. He was fond of it and had put Chidi and me often in trouble in the school when we got involved to revenge for him as a friend, when he got beaten up. Chidi would often tell me, "This is our price for being a friend to a very short man. A short man, a short temper."

"Emeka, why did you march on my cigar?" Obi asked me, his voice a bit raised this time.

I looked at him with the corner of my eyes and pretended paying attention to the orange I was peeling with a small jack penknife. I often stuff some oranges in my pocket to lick when I am whiling away my time, and because of that the small penknife had a permanent place in my pocket.

"It is okay," Chidi said, fetching out a packet of cigarettes from the pocket of his pink trousers. He opened the pack and offered a stick to Obi. Obi sighed as he went nearer to Chidi to collect it.

"He doesn't know the value of it, does he," Obi rhetorically asked, "only because he doesn't smoke?"

It occurred to me, and strangely too, that I was the only non-smoker among us. Chidi had turned Obi into a smoker here at the cemetery with a simple ritual every time we came

51

over here. "Try it, try it, sip it a little, small and small like you are licking a hot soup," Chidi kept encouraging Obi until smoking became Obi's soul mate.

"On the top of the grave," Chidi continued his Ekene's story; Obi was now sitting on a tomb nearer to Chidi than to me, "the skeleton stood. It had patches of decaying fleshes. Maggots were streaming out of its body. Some fell on the ground, climbed up. Some moving from the holes of its eyes and coming out through the mouth. Ekene involuntarily urinated on his blue knickers. The urine ran down his leg, dripping down through the tree branch down to the ground. Ekene prayed that his urine wouldn't betray him. And it looked that way too because the skeleton was more keen to its own mission than being distracted by the eyes of Ekene. The skeleton rested in meditating yoga mood. Ekene battled within himself whether or not to climb down and run back home at that time. Still debating on this decision, when he noticed an intense focalised green light shone on the skeleton. The skeleton began to metamorphose. Layers of flesh were building: the face, stomach, arms and legs were forming. The light suddenly ceased and everywhere became dark. When it became bright again what Ekene saw nearly made him shout."

"What did he see?" Obi asked with a flash of interest on his face.

"A girl, in her early twenties, with a chocolate skin colour, with a Brazilian weavon, wearing yoga black leggings perfectly tighten her, revealing her straight legs and her curved bottom that looked like that of Nicki Minaj. She had a multi coloured slim shirts which tight her lanky body with every contour of her body revealing."

"How about her boob, was it big, pointing out?" I asked, laughing.

The rest joined in my laughter.

"A woman's boob will kill you one day," Obi said amidst his laughter.

"Tell me on earth a man that doesn't like a big breast?" I asked.

"Me," Chidi replied, smiling.

"Oh dear," Obi said, laughing harder. "Chidi tell us what happened next please," he said, waving dismissingly at me to stop me from deviating from the story with the boob talk.

"Ekene was perplexed as he watched the sexy girl," Chidi said. "The girl walked away from the cemetery. Beside the graveyard was a tarred road leading to the town. The girl walked out from the graveyard and stood on the road. Not long a Range Rover passed. She waved the driver of the car but he sped past her, only to reverse later."

"Oh my days," Obi shouted.

"He stopped near her and they began talking," Chidi continued, not caring about Obi's exclamation. "He opened his front door and she entered and they drove off."

"This is exactly what will happen to you, Mr Breast lover," Obi said, giving me an accusing look. "Better stop chasing all those little girls in our school."

"Consolation theology, Mr Morality," I replied. "Don't give yourself any excuse why no girl will agree to go out with you. This story is just a fable. It never happened in the world and will never do."

"This is a real life story," Chidi interjected.

"Says who? Let's not just go to that argument," I said, waving dismissingly at him. "So what happened to Ekene?"

"Ekene?" Chidi rhetorically asked, and continued. "Once the car drove off, Ekene waited a bit more before climbing down the mango tree. By then his body had been hit with a high fever and it was so hot it could boil water to

100 Celsius. Once on the ground, he went over to where he left his brown leather sandals beside the mango trunk to grab it and ran home. Still bending to grab the sandals, he felt somebody tapping him at his back gently. The sandals slipped out of his hand as he turned. The girl was standing at his back."

"What?" Obi screamed feverishly.

"She opened her mouth," Chidi continued without paying attention to Obi's exclamation, "her mouth was filled with six inch nails in the place of teeth. You know those kinds of nails used for roofing? That was the type. And those nails were covered with blood as she opened her mouth widely."

"Mercy," Obi uttered unconsciously, shaking his two legs. And like planned, his word was followed by Chidi's loud fart which had the obnoxious smell of a rotten egg. Obi and I screamed, and jumped up from where we sat, spitting. Chidi was laughing.

"I think that I need to go to do bush method," he said.

"You really need it," I replied, still holding my nose with my left hand and my peeled orange in my right. The knife was in my pocket. "I think you did this on purpose because of your addiction to the bush method."

We all like doing bush method. Sometimes we purposely avoid using our school toilet when pressed in order to defecate in the bush. Obi taught us this defecating pleasure. We would climb a tree whose branches went across the Ngene River. Once on the branch, undies removed, we would excrete, watching how the excreta caused ripples on the water and fishes coming up to feast on it. Obi said that what he enjoyed most on the bush method was how cold breeze licked his anus.

"With this kind of smell from your fart, your faeces are more of a poison to the fish. They will kill all of them," Obi said.

Chidi continued laughing as he walked into the bush through a tiny route we had created from the graveyard to the river. My eyes followed him as he disappeared in the thick forest made up of spear grasses, elephant grasses, palm trees, Agba, cashew trees, and black plum trees that surrounded us. My eyes went around watching the rest of the cemetery. Even though the graveyard wasn't in use, fortunately it kept being cleared and was relatively neat. Chidi said that it was the dead doing the work but I kind of believed Obi who said that it was the purgatorial society, a Roman Catholic group who often pray there on November 2nd of every year, that does the work. Since none of us had witnessed either of the two accounts, it was still a theory.

"What do you think happened to him?" Obi asked me, interrupting my thought.

"Happened to who?"

"Ekene off course."

"I guess the nail teeth woman killed him. What do you think?"

"I don't know but I don't think she wanted him dead. If she did, she would have killed him before driving out with the man in the Range Rover."

"Fair enough. Maybe she can't climb the tree."

Obi laughed. "Ghosts can do anything they want," Obi said.

"Like coming out of their grave now to eat us?"

"Man, stop scaring yourself."

I laughed.

The gathering cloud was beating the sun in the game, sending it to an early retirement for the day. The sky was getting darker each minute and the weather was getting colder. Wind started to blow. The palm trees, Agba, cashew trees, and black plum trees that surrounded us with spear grasses and elephant grasses growing under them were swinging and dancing to and fro to the drum beating of the wind. I guessed that there would be a heavy downpour of rain. Who knows when? And I prayed that it wouldn't be now and wished that the wind would disperse the cloud and prevent the rain from falling.

Obi was busy smoking his cigarette, which he had held onto for long without smoking it. He was humming a song in between the time he would exhale the smoke from his lung before inhaling another one. I couldn't make out which song it was. By then I had long done with the licking of my oranges. And had played the PSG on my phone for a while. When I was getting bored, I checked the time on my watch, it was 5:50 pm. In the next 10 minutes the extramural classes would have dismissed. This was the perfect time for us to sneak back to the school, join the dismissing assembly with the other students like nothing had happened and go home. But with Chidi still on his long business, we would have to wait for a few more minutes.

"Don't you think that Chidi is taking too much time?" Obi asked. It was like he was reading my mind.

"Exactly," I replied.

I watched Obi; his eyes looked blank and distanced like he was in a thought of solving a puzzle. His body was shivering a bit.

"Are you cold?" I asked him.

"Not really, I am thinking about all these ghost stories Chidi told us, and being in a cemetery complicates it more."

"You were encouraging him then, weren't you?"

"Forget about this blame game and let's think of how to get out of here and go home. It is becoming difficult seeing anything now due to darkness and it will soon begin to rain.

None of us will like being under the rain in an open place. And most importantly, I don't like the feelings I am having at present about being here."

The needy childlike voice he used to say this made me laugh so loud. But my laughter was quick to cease when I heard the grasses around us shaking as if somebody was trying to come to where we sat. It was a joy for me at first because I was hoping that it was Chidi but this feeling was replaced with ominous feeling immediately when the sound stopped and there was no Chidi.

"Chidi, stop this game," I said impatiently. "It is dark, cold and windy and will soon rain. We have been waiting for you for ages, let's go home."

No nothing.

I brought out my phone, put on its torchlight, and flashed it in front where the sound came, but saw nobody. I turned the light towards Obi, his shivering was getting worse. It came to my mind that I had not dialled Chidi to know what was still holding him behind. Even if he'd been delivering a baby, the labour had now taken too long.

I scrolled through my phone contacts to where I had saved his number and called.

"The number you are calling at the moment is switched off," the voice of the lady in the automatic machine said. I dialled and dialled again but it was the same response. I asked Obi to do the same, but the number was still switched off. My body grew tense.

What was wrong? Did his battery die? Or was there something else?

"Let's go home," Obi said. "I am feeling weird at the moment. I think something is wrong."

"If something is wrong, that is why we should wait or look for him as a friend," I said.

"Hmmm... you don't understand. This is what neither you nor me can help," Obi replied.

"Be your age. Ghosts and all those stuffs have no real existence, so get over it. You know that it is quite unfair leaving him behind. If it is Chidi, he would not leave you behind."

"I don't care. I just don't feel alright now and don't think I am going to wait any further."

"You are so hypocritical. If Chidi is here now, you will behave like your love for him is as big as the mountain Kilimanjaro."

"Whatever, I am leaving here and going straight home," Obi said with a mean voice.

"Suite yourself," I said.

I saw him walking through the route we came from, murmuring inaudible words. Something I felt sounded like a prayer, a sort of consolation shielding him away from the fear of an attack from an evil spirit. Not long, the abyss of the darkness swallowed the light from his phone.

Inwardly, I felt that it was of no use waiting any further for Chidi at the grave. It had been over an hour since he'd gone to the toilet in the wood. And I was certain that whatever was holding him was anything apart from the answer of nature's call.

I entered the forest through the tiny route we had created down to the river where we climb the tree for defecating. The grasses with the heavy blowing of the wind had come in the way that I could hardly see the track. And the grasses were hitting my eyes, blocking my view, getting on my legs and literally keeping my pace quite slow. I used my left hand to keep them away from my path as much as I could.

I barely had walked for ten minutes in the search for Chidi when the sky opened its eyes and poured its thunderous tears on me. It was accompanied by the flashes of lightning that often blinded my view and horrendous clashes of thunders. My whole body instantly was soaked in the rain. Notwithstanding this, I continued to push on, heading to the river.

At the river bank where we defecate, there was no Chidi. I called for him but the reply I got was the echo of my voice. I decided to walk around the river bank, searching for him. I didn't search for long, though, because the light from my phone suddenly went off. I suspected that my phone might be damaged. Electronics and water were some sort of warring concubines. I shoved the phone back in my pocket to save its remaining life, if at all there was something to salvage from it later.

Without a torchlight, I decided to find my way back home. I thought that that was the best decision for myself. I had reasoned that without any light, I was lost in the belly of the jungle with its ground being slippery and the risk of being attacked by a wild animal, snake or a scorpion, was highly likely. A lot of my classmates at school had often complained that the forest was a den of snakes. For the first time I regretted not listening to Obi.

I staggered through the forest in the narrow and gully-like track we had created and which I believed I was still on. My leg stumbled on a log of wood lying on the ground. I slipped, struggled to maintain my balance but ended up crashing on the ground and the left foot of my sandals slipped off. When I stood up, I felt bruised on my arms and ankles. Since there was no light, I wouldn't know how much I was wounded, although I didn't think that it was a serious injury apart from some scratches.

Blindly, I scrambled, searching for the missing pair of my black sandals. Romancing with the grasses made my body to begin itching. The flashes of lightning and the sound of thunders continued unabated. And it was to my advantage. This was because the lightning became my only source of light. Once it flashed, I quickly memorized the contour of where I was.

I was still trying to locate my lost sandal when the lightning flashed, followed by a cracking thunder, I saw a figure standing not far from me. I raised my head to see clearly, but the darkness that swallowed me immediately after the lightning wouldn't allow me to make out whether I really saw anything out there or whether my imagination was cajoling fun on me.

Even though unconfirmed about what was out there, my heart rate increased and goose bumps ran all over my body. There was another flash of lightning with its accompanying thunder. I looked closer to see whether I was having an unfounded vision. But I was accurate. There was a human, wandering, stumbling for his path. And from the stature of his body and the school uniform he wore, I knew that he was Chidi.

Chidi? Why was he aimlessly walking around, was he touched by an Nju leaf?

I couldn't help but think that Chidi was touched by the leaf. The strange tree in the forest that made people lose their memory, as my mum warned me. And she had said that nobody knew what the tree or its leaf looked like, people only felt its power. The spell from the tree's leaf made people under its possession walk aimlessly in the bush until somebody who knew them called them by their name. My mother had told me a litany of stories of how some people had gone to a forest, encountered it and never came back again. The lucky ones who returned happened to meet somebody they knew in their wandering who recognized them and called them their name. I had never believed any of her story then. I took it as one of those stories that was meant to deter me from exploring the forest aimlessly. But here I was, more than 12 years of hearing such a story and an eye witness to a classical scenario of it.

"Chidi," I called out, walking towards where he was. "One had to hear one's name correctly," mother had said, "before one under such spell can regain consciousness."

Chidi didn't reply.

"Chidi," I called again, "I am Emeka, your friend."

He replied this time around but his response was gibberish and incoherent. But I was inwardly a bit happy. For him to respond at all, it meant that the spell on him was being broken a bit, I thought.

By now, I was getting closer to him with the aid of the light from the lightning which helped me to see him. He had stopped moving around and stood hands akimbo now. I was a few inches away from him.

"Chidi," I said. My hand reached for him. I felt his uneven shoulder. I sensed his uneasiness. "Chidi, what happened to you?"

"Do you know that the Ekene whose tomb you sat on is the same Ekene that met the girl with nail teeth?" Chidi asked me.

His response startled me and sent a chill wave to my spine. For all I expected to hear from him, it wasn't about the ghost story he told us earlier that day. Unconsciously, I withheld my hand from him. My body was tense. I could hear the sound of my heart beats. I felt the need to go to urinate.

"How do you know?" I managed to ask with a voice that sounded too strange even to myself, like a tape stocked to a stereo.

"I saw him," Chidi said.

When he said this, there was a sudden change in his eyes which started radiating with a greenish light. And I saw his teeth too. They were all six inch nails, sharpened and pierced, neatly arranged without a space in his mouth. He tried to reach for my hand. I didn't know how but my hand went straight to the little knife in my pocket and I stabbed him in the chest. He screamed a hellish scream. It was like an echo, reverberating back, merging the past and the future into a scary present. I took to flight. And he began to pursue me.

I ran blindly through the bush, pushing away grasses blocking my path as swift as I could. At this time, the rain had stopped falling but the ground was wet, some places with a flood of water. My leg waggled through those floods, splashing muddy water all over my body. But right then being clean was a luxury I didn't give a damn about. I took glances at my back as I ran, hoping to catch a glimpse of him chasing me but all I could see was an ocean of darkness. I had to rely on my hearing to pick the sound made by his body as he struggled through the forest too.

I couldn't remember how long I had run, maybe an hour or so when I stopped hearing him pursuing me. But I didn't give up pushing ahead. I hoped that as long as I kept moving ahead, not only would I be far from his reach but I could stumble upon a person, road or anything that could help me get home.

And I was right. I hadn't run for more than 10 minutes when I saw a torchlight flashing in front of me. With the little energy left in me, I screamed for help and ran as fast as I could to the source of light.

"Help me… help me," I pleaded, panting.

The light was on my face as I was running closer, now on

a tarred road.

"Emeka, what is wrong?"

I could recognise the voice and it was the last thing I had expected to hear. Obi? Didn't he go home? What was happening tonight?

I halted at a spot. "Didn't you go home, Obi? Why are you here?"

"Answer me first: what is chasing you?"

"You have to answer me," I yelled, and was growing suspicious of him, walking back little by little.

"When I left you and was walking to the school," Obi said, "I started hearing wolfish sounds in front of me inside the bush. I became afraid and couldn't continue on that path. I had to return back to the cemetery and walked through the eastern side of our route, still hoping to find our school. It was how I got myself lost and at the end stumbled on this tarred road. I have been following it ever since, hoping to arrive at a place I can see help or see anybody driving or walking by."

As he was saying this, he was coming closer to me. From the reflection of the light from his phone, I could see his shivering body. It sort of comforted me because it still reflected the panicking Obi I knew. And more so, he was unlike Chidi when I saw him, who looked like everything remained the same.

But how did Obi's phone withstand the rain?

"But why were you running?" Obi asked me, interrupting my thought. He was standing in front of me now.

I told him everything that had happened in the forest: how I met Chidi, what he told me about Ekene, and how he transformed and all that.

"We need to run away from here," I told him. "He may

be somewhere looking for me now."

Obi's right hand held my left hand firmly. I was amazed about that and more about how strong his hand was. His trembling body had gone. My eyes met his. They were already glowing with a green light.

"Are his teeth like this?" Obi asked me.

I saw the nail teeth and before I could struggle out from his grab, the teeth went deep into my neck.

I was breathless, I was slipping away.

*

"Why did you bring me to a cemetery?" I asked Ifeanyi.

"Doesn't it look cool? Think of staging a night party here away from the tons of eyes of anybody?"

I felt spooky about this graveyard but thinking of having a wild party here with my girlfriend and the liberty to have enough booze and drug was a temptation I couldn't resist. And to imagine also that I could have sex in a different setting than I was used to was watering my mouth.

"I have heard a story of three students that came here years ago and went missing."

"That is a myth. I don't believe in fabricated fables," Ifeanyi replied.

"You may be right," I said. "Our culture is too superstitious and people scare themselves a lot."

"True, and besides, I can't see any connection between their missing with this serene abandoned cemetery," Ifeanyi said. He then sat in a tomb with the epitaph Ekene Okoro (1970-1985).

"Are you in?" he asked.

"Yes," I answered as I went to sit in a nearby tomb beside him.

64

To Love is Strange

"You are free to have sex but never with someone you have loved. That is our curse," my mum told me in the dawn of my adolescence. So when I started seeing Ebuka, I knew that it would end like that story Mama told me in the wake of my puberty or like that of my father whom I never met.

It wasn't like I didn't try to keep to my mother's advice. I did with all my strength. For instance, back then in the University of Nigeria, Nsukka, when what all those around me were doing was to find a partner, kissing like pigeons, holding hands, smooching and cuddling especially at night in the dark corners around Lady Ibiam, Isa-Kata, Awolowo and other female hostels. I stumbled upon a lot of those sights, with their silhouette outlines, whenever I was returning from the library. It was one of the reasons I preferred to study in my room. I had built my wall to keep myself away from those feelings of wanting to own a man. And if I had a body need, I knew how to lock myself up in the bathroom, lie on the shower tab and touch myself, handheld showerhead always handy.

That wall shielded Ebuka away from me then, when I first saw him. But it wasn't that I hadn't loved him inwardly. In fact it was nothing but my love for him that made me refuse to confess my feelings to him. I knew what repercussion it would hold for me as well as for him if I had.

But what kind of a girl would see Ebuka and wouldn't blush? The sporty Ebuka, six foot tall, with athletic build and rounded muscles on his shoulders and legs, sporting wavy hair and an ebony skin. He was the first I had fallen for, so to say, except my secondary school days' guys I ended up kissing, fondling for fun, but had never wanted to have any of them the way I craved for Ebuka. When I first saw Ebuka, I was living at the Hilltop, at the outskirts of the university. I didn't live in the campus hostels. I hated school hostels. The memories of my secondary school dormitory, its dirtiness, rowdy, noisy and nosey characters was suffocating and put to coffin any idea of living in a communal environ again. Ebuka happened to be living in the next house in front of my studio apartment. My room was in the first floor of a yellow building, facing an untarred road leading the residents to the market, the Uni and virtually to all other connections to the outside world. I had one hobby then and even now, and that was human-watching. My twin sister Juliet said that I was a compulsive gossiper. I didn't know what she meant by that, but having an access to where I could observe human beings chatting, playing, rushing, laughing and all that, in a natural state and not with a defensive mechanism of knowing that they were being watched was priceless and fun for me. I crave for it obsessively like cigarette addicts do to smoking.

With my mug of hot Lipton tea at the window, I would watch people on their workaday life. I couldn't remember what made me have a sleepless night on the day I saw Ebuka, but I had gone to the window early that morning to kill time and boredom. In his blue sports shorts, grey sleeveless Nike sport shirt, blue trainers, Ebuka was running the track. My jaw dropped open, my heart ceased to beat, and moistures appeared on my palms. I suddenly began to feel wet under my armpit. I couldn't take my staring away from him until he disappeared from my view. It soon became my regular routine to stand in that window that faced the untarred road in front of my house every morning waiting to see Ebuka joggle by. Then I would imagine all the fantasies of how his warm body could feel to mine and how his aftershave would be smelling on my pillow afterwards and how I would be putting on his t-shirts, which would be oversize to me, posing for him in hot pants.

I was still perfecting my plans on how I would make him notice me and chase me when my twin sister, Juliet, called me and informed me of our aunt, Ngozi, who the doctor said had only twenty-four hours to live. My aunt had been hidden from public eyes for fifteen years now by our clan due to her ill health. Last month she was taken to the hospital as part of the ritual cleanse by the clan for her being under the curse. Although I don't know the rationale for bringing her to the hospital at all during her last moments, it was our duty to pay her a last homage before her death. All of us knew why she was suffering. She had loved a man and knew within her heart that she did and went ahead to have sex with him and had even made a baby with him. Although none of us young ones knew the man, I even doubt that my older aunts have the knowledge of who he was too, but I was only certain of one thing, that the said man wasn't alive anymore. And nobody tried to give a thought to how he died because thinking such a thought was like digging into what happened to the father of any of us in the clan, assuming that our mum loved our daddy before we were conceived. With the rest of the family, I had gone to say a final farewell to Aunty Ngozi. I saw how our aunt, dressed in the hospital green gown, lay on the bed like a feeble and tattered rag, pallid, and stomach swollen like a child suffering from kwashiorkor. She had a rotten odour like cow dung and even the smell of antiseptic nurses were pouring every other ten minutes on her couldn't neutralise it. And that was the only treatment the hospital could provide since every other doctor had said that scientifically nothing was wrong with my aunt based on the labs tests conducted. Seeing all these, the feelings I had about Ebuka vanished immediately. By the end of the semester, I found a new place at Odim gate, about 15 miles from Hilltop, so that Ebuka could move out of my sight and mind and then from my yearning for him forever.

But this wasn't to be so. I met Ebuka again.

This time I was a stock broker with the Union Bank at Ofuluonu. Anyway, I saw Ebuka in an unrelated place to my job.

My twin Juliet, drama queen, coffee skin and slender in shape, brought the idea of attending church to me at first. We were going for grocery shopping at Ogige market, she was driving in her yellow Toyota Camry when she began complaining that she needed sex, proper one where she could really play with a man's stuff, and not the one she could do by using Rabbit pearl, Form 3 or Handheld showerhead. As she was saying that, she was rolling her eyes and kept smacking her lips and hitting her hands in the steering wheel like she was drunk or being controlled by cocaine. Because it was a Friday, I had told her to wait for the next day, she could go to club at Enugu but she should know that I wasn't coming with her. She laughed and told me that she had another place of getting men for flinging without bothering to travel miles away, which we do for clubbing when we needed a bed mate. The idea of travelling miles for no-string attached casual sex was hers too. She needed it to be as discrete as possible. Ofuluonu, the community where we lived, was so closely knit together that people scoop and gossip about each other's life and even about the life of any stranger on a visit. As Juliet often said, "Ofuluonu village knew even the whereabouts of each of the cockroaches in her vicinity." I questioned Juliet about how such a close range sex mate could blow our cover. But she assured me that we were well protected under the umbrella of the people of God.

"Ginika, people look at anything that goes between us and our bed mate as an accepted relationship between a church brother and a sister," Juliet said, laughing, smacking her palms further at the steering and shaking her head. Her braids with extension rolled in front of her face, covering her eyes. She shook her head again, sending them backwards.

I joined her in her laughing too.

"You see… their pastors have a better flinging than most of us get," Juliet said. "Guess who smashed me first?" Juliet asked me.

I waved my head in a negation.

"It was their assistant head pastor. A married man. You see, it is a win-win situation."

I laughed.

The next day was a Saturday and I spent it shopping at Ogige market looking for the best outfit for my man-hunting the day next. It was sunny and it made me sweat. I don't like shopping under the sun at Ogige market, especially on Saturdays because it was often crowded. People fluttered like flies at the passages connecting different shops as they priced and bought. People rubbed each other with their sweat as they bumped into one another. The noise produced was horrendous. But due to my mission the next day, I had no option than to go. Juliet had admonished that I had to be classy, flamboyant and sexy but not too provocative.

"Church guys," Juliet said over the phone, "are entrapped in the world of dreaming to be wild but are caged in the prison of conservatives. They are tricky at times."

At the end, I settled for a black short-sleeved jumpsuit. I would have preferred a white one I saw but I didn't pick it because it had an open back. Juliet's advice was a torchlight to my shopping taste.

Juliet came to pick me up from my flat on the Sunday where I was living at Manu's quarter in Ofuluonu. Her bungalow house was about ten minutes' drive from mine. After our secondary school days, when we had quarrelled and reconciled and quarrelled again to reconcile, we discovered that even though we could not live without each other, we could not stay under the same roof together for weeks without getting on each other's nerve. Her showcasing, domineering, and sometimes rude character pissed me off. But to be honest, she was all I wanted to be: a proper badass.

Juliet was wearing an indigo Lovedrobe Maxi High Low Hem dress matching with violet high heels. Her eyelashes and lips were done the same colour. Immediately I saw her I felt grumpy and old. But Juliet's compliments on my jumpsuit, which I felt were sincere, revived me and gave me confidence.

In the church, I sat beside Juliet in the pew. Throughout the service we gossiped in drowned whispers.

Juliet said, rolling her eyeballs at my left, "Look at that guy in the blue suit, sitting four pews from us on your left, he is cute. I like his hair style and body build too. I think he will be my catch today."

"How will you get him?"

"Just watch me."

Juliet showed me the assistant pastor that she first slept with when she began worshipping here. He was in his early forties and kept his beard and moustache trimmed. He was wearing a black suite with a bow tie. He had a boyish smile which he kept flashing when he was giving the church announcement.

"Is he not hot?" Juliet asked me in a whispering voice.

I nodded my head in agreement although inwardly I felt

that he was too old for Juliet.

"You can have him too," she said, smiling and smacking my shoulder.

I couldn't help but think how many men Juliet had slept with in the church and here I was sexually starved.

When the church service was about to end, the pastor invited all the first timers to come to the altar. There were three of us. Two elderly women in their late forties. One was putting on a purple gown whereas the other wore blue jean trousers and a milk polo top. The church choir sang *You Are Welcome in the Name of the Lord* for us and the pastor prayed for us asking God that we should be established in their church. Later, the usher led us through the aisle of the church to the back of the building to meet the welcoming team. The service was brought to an end as we moved to the back of the church.

Four people came to welcome us, three women and a man. The man among the team was Ebuka. The five years that had gone by didn't affect Ebuka's look in any way. He was still with his dandy look, his glittering eyes, and his broad smile. His athletic body was still intact too. Immediately I saw him, I missed my step, shyness descended on me and my heart fluttered. I was blushing.

"God, I hope that I am not still in love with him?" I thought aloud.

Throughout the time the team was talking to us and encouraging us for coming to be part of the family of Christ Embassy, my mind wasn't in there. I kept looking at Ebuka from the corner of my eyes, my heart beat escalating and I was feeling hot and weak. My eyes sometimes interlocked with that of Ebuka. I did observe from the corner of my eyes also that he was staring at me. This fact made me uncomfortable and curious.

"Do I know you from somewhere?" Ebuka asked, smiling.

By then the welcoming team had dismissed us with a booklet of *Rhapsody* by the church founder. I was still in the church using my eyes to search where Juliet was. Majority of the congregation had gone home, leaving three groups that were having their meeting at three separate locations inside the church hall. Juliet was in one of the groups. I suspected that it was the choristers because in front of where they sat discussing were bands, guitars, piano and some other musical instruments I don't know their names. Juliet was sitting with the guy she had shown me. They were whispering as the choir meeting was going on.

"Yes, of course, you lived not far from my house five years ago," I felt like telling Ebuka but I didn't.

"I don't know," I replied to him.

"Where did you attend your Uni?" Ebuka asked me.

"University of Nigeria, Nsukka."

"I thought so," he said, smiling, clasping his hand. "When I was looking at you I was quite sure that I had met you before but I couldn't tell where exactly. Can I know your pretty name again?"

"Ginika."

"Yes, I can remember. Your name is as beautiful as you are anyway."

"Thank you."

"You are welcome. By the way I am Ebuka."

I wanted to tell him that I knew him, that I had done a bit of a background inquiry on him five years ago. But I didn't. I was afraid of sounding too desperate.

At that time the choristers dismissed from their meeting. I saw Juliet discussing with her new catch, walking towards us.

"That is my sister coming, I am going to meet her now."

"It is alright. Can we keep in touch please? Can we exchange phone contacts?"

"Yes, of course."

Ebuka later left to join another group still meeting at the far end of the church hall. They were up to fifteen members and seemed to be absorbed with whatever they were discussing. I took my glance towards the choir stand. Juliet with her new man stood at a point discussing.

I took a deep breath. I was having an ambivalent feeling about Ebuka. What was I walking into? Isn't this suicide? I knew that deep within me right now I was not supposed to have sex with Ebuka. I had feelings for him and doing it with him meant my dying like aunt one day. And his lot would be worse.

My thought was interrupted when I saw Juliet coming towards me beaming with happiness like she had won a lotto.

"I told you I would get him," Juliet said triumphantly, nudging me. We were walking now to where she parked her car in a football pitch in front of the church. The parking space of the church was too little to accommodate the cars of its teaming population, so the congregation converted a soccer pitch behind the church into a second car park. The pitch had patches of green grasses on it. Those grasses in the pitch looked like the only surviving hair in a bald man's head.

"How did you get him?" I asked Juliet.

"After the service, I walked to him, pestered him to be a member of the choir and he agreed." Juliet winked at me. "The rest is history," Juliet said. "By the way, after your foundation classes as a new member of the church, you will join either the choristers or the ushers. That is where you can catch men easily. Don't worry about being active, I am not," she said, laughing.

"I will remember that."

"You don't sound happy. Don't you like it here?"

"I am just thinking how you manage to be having sex with men you see constantly and still manage not to be in love with them? I can understand party flinging but not this one."

"It is simple. I just sleep with each man once. After that, I am done with the person. I will delete the person's contact from my phone and block the person. Sex is sex for me, it is fun. Our body needs it just like we need food. But love is a deceptive construct the human mind built to ensnare itself. I don't give a damn about it, I don't need that prison."

I was surprised to see how Juliet had adapted her life to mirror exactly the curse laid on our clan: have sex but don't love. And these gave her a lot of freedom and carefree life to explore like a teenager. But being a one-man woman was a terrible chill to me. It was this, perhaps, more than the fact that Enugu was far, made me abhor going to club, catch up with a random guy, and sex at the slightest convenient place: inside the toilet, in the car or lying at its bonnet or just bending over at a corner in the street.

The same day at night, Ebuka texted me. He was asking how I found the church service and other stuffs I couldn't remember now. But I did still remember his last text when he was wishing me goodnight. He wrote: "I sent the angels to take care of you as you sleep but they came back to me telling me that angels don't guide an angel. Sweet dreams angel Ginika." The text blew me off then but I later discovered that the text was copied from somewhere else when I saw a similar text in Juliet's phone from another admirer of hers.

Ebuka's texts kept flooding. I replied sparely, not because I wanted to test him first and see how much his patience span would last but because I knew that I had fallen for him and that was no good for either of us. Most often I kept my reply to him to the barest minimum. Frequently I texted words like "ok, yes, cool, alright" as my reply to his litany of words. Ebuka later told me that he made up a name for me then, 'one word girl'.

Juliet called me on Thursday to tell me that her new catch had slept with her. Her voice rang like a child's. She went on to describe the sex scene which took place on the sofa.

"He is a good kisser," Juliet said, and laughing, "and a professional with oral sex, my weakness."

I asked her the fate of the guy and she told me that she had deleted and blocked his number immediately she came out of his house.

I skipped church that Sunday because I didn't want to see Ebuka. On the Saturday night he texted asking me whether I would come to church and that he wouldn't mind offering me a lift. I just replied, "Maybe." Early Sunday morning, I turned off my phone only to turn it on later when I knew it was too late for him to pick me up. Immediately I turned on the phone, voicemail alerts showing his six missed calls came in. After the Sunday service he texted and inquired what happened that made me unable to attend the service. I replied, "Sick." Earlier, I told Juliet that I wouldn't be able to go to the church with her because I had a backlog of urgent work in my office so I had to give up my Sunday service.

"Good girl," she said at the other end of her phone, "make sure that they pay you overtime."

I accepted Ebuka's date three weeks after I first saw him in the church. During these three weeks he was constantly chatting me up until I succumbed. Inwardly I knew that I was taking a risk but being lonely was depressive. Even though I was close to my sister, she had her own life, often busy at the hospital where she worked as a nurse. Besides that, I knew that her perception of life differed greatly from mine and made it difficult for me to tell her everything about myself. Should I, for instance, tell her about Ebuka, she would never understand me and we would argue for ages. That was of no use for me now, it would end up sapping my energy and make me feel pathetic, stupid and worst of whatever I was feeling right now. My mother was the last to come to my mind as somebody to make me feel less lonely. Each day she grew more distanced, her mind cast away into an impenetrable shore. Even though she was young, still in her late forties, grey hair had started to sprout on her head and she hardly took care of herself. Juliet and I knew that she was fighting a battle but she never wanted to let any of us into the matter.

For our first date, Ebuka took me to a cinema at Amachara to watch *Half of a Yellow Sun*, a novel turned movie. Ebuka was a pro-Biafran so I understood why he wanted to see the movie which was on the Biafra war. I read the novel which I really loved. My curiosity was to see how the adaptation was. Inside the cinema, which was half full with people, and lights turned off, I didn't much follow the storyline of the movie. This was because Ebuka was so eager and his hand throughout the show was working on me. He was smoothing my palms, caressing, squeezing my bottom and rubbing my laps. His hand sent my concentration on holiday to the land of fantasy. It was in the cinema that we first kissed. That night at his house, we made love.

After that night that I laid naked with him on his bed with his strong arms holding me tight, I became worried about him. Each minute I lived in fear waiting for when he would call to tell me that he was sick. Once he complained about a malaria and for the next three days it took him to be well again I was literally pissing on myself. During my free times I spent it on Google and in medical library digging to know if I could see anything relating to curse and the sickness I knew would befall him soon. All these I kept away from Ebuka as I still opened my arms for his endless love.

I was planning to travel with Ebuka to Enugu the next day for shopping but Juliet called me.

"Mummy is sick and is suffering from that," Juliet said.

Juliet believed that I should know what she meant by 'that', and actually I did.

It was not that Juliet was afraid that somebody might be intercepting our call but she was ashamed of what our mother had just become. 'That' cursed sick woman that should be quarantined as she waits patiently for her death. Obviously we two would share from her shame among our clan. I knew how Ngozi's daughter avoided every occasion organised by the clan because of the look and the taunt she was getting. Her name and description was reduced to a sick woman's daughter.

Juliet was pissed more because she thought that our conception came from one-night stand. The way our mother had absconded from talking about whoever our father was pointed to me that she had a secret that she was hiding. By the way, having a child by one-night stand was the proper ethics in our clan and nobody was ashamed of it. Every one of our mums was a single mother.

I cancelled my shopping with Ebuka and lied to him that I had an emergency in the office. He fumed under rage and told me to tell my boss that I had a life.

"Life is not work… work… work… work," he said.

I told him that I would remember it next time. He cut the

phone in annoyance.

The next day I travelled with Juliet to visit our mother. She lived at Opi, a town at the outskirt of where we lived in Ofuluonu. It was five miles to be precise. We went in my Red Honda jeep. I was driving. Juliet had told me on the phone that she wasn't in the best mood to ride. I knew that whatever made Juliet give up being the driver when one was travelling with her was quite serious.

Juliet was wearing a plain purple gown without any makeup. It was the first time as an adult I could remember not seeing her in makeup. Three months later when I went to see her corpse and her suicide note: *love is strange, not to love is strange,* she was wearing makeup lying in a bathtub after slicing open her vein and bleeding to death before her housekeeper discovered her corpse.

Juliet was sitting beside me, the car window was down and she was complaining about every single thing: my car had a lot of air-freshener smell in it, the road had a lot of potholes, and other cars driving through were speeding. She was everything I knew apart from Juliet. Her cheerfulness had gone, her eyes looked like she hadn't slept for weeks. She was like an isolated building, decaying and falling. I knew that the news of our mother haunted her so much but I didn't expect her to change within a day. Perhaps she thought that Mother didn't care about men, so she had anchored her as her role model. Now the foundation had been shaken and she was struggling to adapt.

To think of how I survived those moments puzzles me even now. I had more worries than Juliet. Apart from Mother and whatever headache would come from the fact that she was sick, the implication of my relationship with Ebuka was a burden. It pained me constantly to know that he could suddenly die in a tragic way I don't even know. And then I had to carry the guilty conscience that I killed him because of my personal greed to be loved. That I would die like Aunt Ngozi or like our mother was about to die was the least of my headache.

I paid deaf ears to Juliet's whinging. I was thinking of my own world.

"I hope that you have not fallen in love too?" Juliet asked me from the blues. Her eyes were on me. I avoided it by staring straight into the long road ahead.

The question startled me. I was not prepared for it, at least not now. I knew that I had kept my relationship away from the gaze of everybody. I had for one thing prevented Ebuka from visiting me. I told him that I lived with my family and was not ready to introduce him to any member of my family until I was sure that he was the one for me. He had insisted and argued but I told him to quit his coaching job as proof of his seriousness but he called me a joke. He later nicknamed me 'ghost lady' and told me that the name was a replacement for the former 'one word girl'. I laughed. Whenever we wanted to see each other, I would drive to his house at Nru, which was about four kilometres from mine, and from there we would head to wherever we wanted to go.

"Why did you ask me such a question?" I asked Juliet.

"C'mon, give me yes or no as an answer. Why are you beating around the bush?" Juliet asked me as she brought out a handkerchief from her purse to sneeze.

"Until you tell me why you asked that question, I am not telling you anything."

"It is obvious that you are seeing somebody. That is why you hardly have time for me anymore."

"I have told you over and over again that my work is getting harder."

"This is a super story," Juliet taunted.

"Believe whatever you want, it is not my headache."

I never knew that Juliet would notice the way she did and interpret my sudden infrequency from those activities that brought us together as a sign of me seeing a man. Since Ebuka began dating me, occasions had risen when Juliet needed to hang out with me and it happened that Ebuka needed my attention too and Juliet's was always sacrificed.

We drove for the rest of the journey in silence. Often I took a glance at Juliet, her eyes fixed outside the window like a troubled teenager.

Mummy was sitting in the red sofa in the living room watching NTA news when we came in. She regarded us as she reduced the volume of the TV with her remote. Her physique was intact: her chubby body, plump cheeks, and glittering eyes. But the odour oozing out of her was like that of decayed rotten meat. My stomached turned and I felt like vomiting. I watched Juliet from the corner of my eyes gasping for air.

While I was coming, I thought I would use the chance to ask Mother a lot of things, about Father, how he died and something intimate that could give me a clue as to what might happen to Ebuka. But the present state she was in made my head run *tabular-raza*.

Juliet and I were in the living room for up to an hour, neither of us speaking, as if somebody was dead. Mother kept gazing at the TV without its sound for about thirty minutes before turning it off and heading to her bedroom. Juliet cupped her head on her hand and later fell asleep on the sofa. My eyes were just darting to and fro. When she woke up, she tapped me and signalled to me that it was time to go home.

That was the last time of seeing Mummy together with

80

Juliet because the next day the clan came and carted her away. They dumped her in the sanctuary where she would stay and undergo her decaying process. Apart from the ones involved in the rituals of that moment, she was excluded from the rest of society. The next time she would be due to be seen was when it would be about a month of her death. The clan would keep her in a hospital where the rest of her family members would come to pay their last respect. Many years before this time came for Mummy, Juliet's body was discovered by her housekeeper on the sink with her suicide note.

Fifteen years later, I would talk about this moment with Mother when I was paying my last respect to her with my daughter, Ifeoma. I had asked Mother to forgive my naiveté, to forgive my silence when my voice and support was needed most. I had allowed the shame of what I felt she had become to make me forget all that she was to me. We wailed together and a flood of tears soaked our bodies. Later she kissed Ifeoma on her cheek and we waved goodbye only for her to die the next day, two days earlier than the doctor had estimated.

Outside, beside my car, Juliet vomited. I was surprised that I didn't vomit too. I helped her cover the vomit with sand. We drove off. Throughout the journey, I kept spitting on my handkerchief. My stomach was really upset. Juliet spat also but not as much as I did. She spat through the window onto the road.

Juliet told me that she had an appointment with a hair dresser that evening but felt right now that she wasn't in the mood anymore. She had to cancel it. Her phone battery was down so she asked for my phone to make the call. I took it from the pigeon hole and gave it to her. She made the call and successfully cancelled the appointment, although I could overhear the disappointed voice from the other end. Juliet didn't return my phone immediately. I thought that she was playing with it, without knowing that she was reading my text messages with Ebuka.

"So you lied to me," Juliet said. "You have a man."

"What is wrong with you?"

"Who is Ebuka?"

I was shocked to hear that name but when I saw her staring at my phone and obviously at my texts with Ebuka, I knew that there was no more point dragging and lying about it.

"Yes, I am seeing him and it is my choice. Tell me nothing about it because I won't listen."

Juliet raged and started swearing at me. Throughout our journey till I dropped her off at hers, we were arguing and verbally abusing each other. That was my last time of seeing Juliet and talking with her before she died. Two weeks later I tried talking with her but her phone was switched off. I tried on different days and still got the same answer. I gave up. I concluded that she had changed her phone number and didn't want me to be in contact.

Anyway, before I received the news of her suicide, I had another emotional blow. Ebuka's sickness began. Ebuka returned from his Saturday coaching earlier than usual. Most often my Saturdays are in his. He complained of a headache splitting his head. I bought Panadol for him to take. Before evening that day, he was crying like a baby. His body temperature was hot like the scourge of a Harmattan sun. I took him to the hospital. All the drugs he took amounted to nothing. His blood, urine and faeces were taken to a laboratory for a test. The result came that he was healthy. Within two weeks I tried four different hospitals with him, but the result was the same. Ebuka was medically healthy but physically dying. On the third week of his illness, his penis and its surrounding began decaying with maggots pumping out. It was then that I knew that hospital was no good for him, the curse was taking its toll. I brought him home, and decided to nurse him on my own, to walk with him in his last moments. That was unfortunately all the remedy I could offer him for bringing this doom on him.

When Ifeoma my daughter reached her puberty, I told her every truth surrounding her birth. I didn't know what decision she would later make, to love or not to love. But whatever course she takes, there is no safe route, each are precariously marred. As Juliet rightly put it in her suicide note:

To love is strange
Not to love is strange.

A CURSED CITY

Its appearance was mysterious, sudden and hellish, just like the havoc and trauma it began causing. And before we could fashion out what we would do, the missing rate of our children had escalated to at least three persons per day.

The first to report its appearance didn't help the matter – or should I rather say we didn't? Perhaps it was her personality – a woman drunkard – that made us not listen. We, the king's cabinet don't stand such a sight: haggard, shabby, with swollen eyes, standing in the king's court talking to us, God forbid! Or was it her history, the secret of our collective survival, but, above all, our collective guilty conscience that made us pay deaf ears to the glaring truth? But, all those times she was telling us about that strange winged creature she saw, my mind was reminiscing her past beautiful body; the sexy body that was my fantasy. My wife once complained that when I made love to her, in my ecstasy I called Nkechi. I didn't believe that. But here is the Nkechi, a ghost of herself. Who would still believe that this was the girl whose beauty nearly drove me mad in the last fifteen years? The girl because of whom I leave my hut at night and trek for at least a mile to hers in order to hide in the bush waiting for when she would be taking her bath so that I could peep through the bamboo bathroom? Anyway, it wasn't like I planned this falling in love, it just happened. I was returning from a friend's house the night it occurred; I walked across to her house, saw her naked body in the rays of the lantern radiating from her bathroom… the deal was done. The lusting began.

We dismissed her as a drunkard. But before then, one of us asked her to describe the winged animal she saw. She said that it had a raven's head, legs and wings, but with a human trunk. And it flew with great speed. The sarcastic question that followed was that if the speed was such, how did she manage to see all these details? When she was mumbling out words to defend herself, rolls of laughter from us swallowed her voice. Then another asked her whether or not she had taken some palm wine before the incident happened. In anger, she left us.

We later went home. But not up to an hour at our house, the emergency court gong was sounded. We rushed back. The king was already seated on his throne wearing a sad and panicking face. Beside him stood a woman about forty years of age. She was tying a red wrapper marked with white strips. Her eyes were swollen and reddish, caused by an excessive shedding of tears. Tears were still flowing down her cheeks as she made effort to control her emotions. Her husband, with a loincloth over his waist and a bare chest, stood mouth agape and mind faraway. Nobody exchanged any pleasantry as each made for his seat. When the king saw that a quorum had been formed, he began with the customary greeting, although this time all its flavour had waded away.

"Just a few hours after you left," he continued after the greeting, "this woman and her husband rushed to my court, wailing. My attendants calmed them down before admitting them to my presence. When they came in, I asked them what was it, and they told me a story I never had heard since I was born in this town, Diogbe."

He paused, coughed and swallowed some saliva. He majestically adjusted himself in the throne and then turned to face the wailing woman and her husband. "Mrs. Ada," he continued, "stories are better told in the mouths of the people who witnessed it first. You should tell my cabinet what you said happened to you."

Immediately she opened her mouth to speak the suppressed crying emerged. Tears were flowing down, painting the mud floor wet. Her husband came near her and used his right hand to pull her closer to himself. He began consoling her, cleaning her tears with his palms. But he couldn't control his own emotions, and tears began gushing out from his eyes like a fast river.

We watched the melodrama. Ojemba, the chief security officer of the king, was the first person to interrupt this unabashed expression of emotion. All of us later caught on that and shouted on the couple to spare us from their uncontrolled feelings.

"This was my only child I had after my fifteen years of fruitless marriage," the woman said amidst her sobbing.

"And so what?" I saw myself nearly asking her but Ojemba had the right lexis for the situation. "Madam, if you want us to solve this problem, I don't think your crying would help the matter. The more you waste time crying, the more you delay the time we could have used to take a decision on what to do pertaining the issue of your son."

This speech did the miracle and spared us from further embarrassment. She quickly put herself together.

"I was farming behind my hut," she began. "My husband wasn't there. He had gone to our main farm at Amaofor. My son was alone playing in front of my hut. That was how I left him before entering into the farm. I heard him scream. I left what I was doing and rushed out. When I came in front of my hut, I didn't see any trace of my son. He had vanished."

"Vanished to where?" Ojemba asked.

"I don't know."

"Did you search for him?"

"Yes, I did. I searched inside my hut, that of my husband and our kitchen but he wasn't there. I searched also around the bushes surrounding our house. Even though I was sure it was his scream I heard, I had to look around the neighbourhood to make sure he wasn't there. And I did not see him."

"Did you check his close friend's house?"

Mrs. Ada kept quiet.

"I asked this," Ojemba continued, "because it is possible it isn't his scream you heard. Remember this is your only child and so you worry much for him. Your imagination may be playing a trick on you. You think you heard a sound without knowing that it was all made up from your wild thinking."

"I did later check. It was after that did I rush to our farm to tell my husband what happened."

I then asked her whether she saw any mark on the ground; footprints and stuff like that. She said that she was heartbroken, confused and devastated to look out for such details. I pinpointed to her that it was necessary to look out for such, because whatever would make her son disappear as she claimed must leave marks.

We later sent them home. The king promised them that a searching team would be dispatched to look for their son across our kingdom and even beyond.

Immediately they left, two women came, crying. They wanted to see the king as a matter of urgency. We guessed what the content of the complaint would turn out to be: another case of missing children.

The king adjusted himself in his throne. "I think that he has come for his revenge," he said.

None of us replied until he soliloquised it loudly again. I

had to reply. I knew I had to because I was central to this. And at this point in time, I couldn't let him seem so abandoned, so depressed on what we collectively did. I knew that it would be against his name. It would be written in the book of history that it was during his reign that the mighty Diogbe dynasty, which had lasted for over a century, had fallen. A depressing responsibility to shoulder. But I too wouldn't like to see such happen in my own days. It was this precisely that never made me to think twice on agreeing to that human sacrifice, knowing too well its precarious nature, especially during this time when the running of our kingdom was being interfered with by the Whiteman's administration, who had established their base at our neighbouring kingdom, Umunko. But then the wrath of our ancestors was a worse alternative to face if we evaded the sacrifice.

Uzodima, our past king was dead. Prince Chidi, the present king came to me at night the same day, paled. He disclosed to me the fear he would have in giving his father a befitting royal burial. That fear was genuine; the Whiteman had recently abolished human sacrifice. For a king to be properly buried in our custom, his body had to be laid to rest with two human heads, an adult male and that of a child. This custom had been there before we were born and according to our ancestors it was conducted uninterruptedly for all time. But now, in our time, it was a different ball game.

"Every life is a life," the Whiteman had insisted the day he abolished human sacrifice, "and should be treated with equal respect. None should be used for a ritual for the sake of the so-called supreme one. Disobedience to this merits death penalty to any person or group caught doing it."

No person doubted the seriousness of the Whiteman. The bloody war they waged with Umunko's dynasty over tax issue showed us the powerfulness of their weaponry, and deposited in us fear to avoid any confrontation with them.

That notwithstanding, I couldn't bear seeing our custom whisked away just like that. Probably, it may be, this passion had Chidi seen in me displayed in the court during the time of his father that made him seek me out among the entire king's cabinet at this crucial issue.

"I can't say much for now," I told him, "but what I can promise is that none of our customs will be compromised."

The next day, I began lobbying and negotiating with other members of the cabinet. Luckily, all concurred that they would stand by the tradition we inherited from our ancestors. But the problem now was how to get that head without attracting the attention of the Whiteman.

In the bygone days, getting a head was difficult but not as it was now. With the death of any king, all their neighbouring villagers would be on the lookout, because they knew kidnappers soon would be on rampage scouting for the two heads. Parents at that time didn't send their ward on an errand and people tended to move in group. And then each would be listening to know when the unlucky victim would be caught. It was a time for endless rumour and speculations. Who and who escaped the kidnappers? Who and who was caught? The end of which was when the kingdom would fix the burial ceremony of their king. That implied that the unfortunate victims had been caught. The kidnappers themselves didn't find the job funny. They were trending in a precarious job. If they became unfortunate and were caught by any of the neighbouring kingdoms, their legs and hands would be chopped off and put inside their bags. The bag then would be tied around their necks. They would be sent home. Many died on the road due to excess bleeding. And that was a food for the vulture.

It was Ojemba who suggested a way we could follow to reduce security risk. According him, "Kidnapping a third party from another kingdom definitely means sending a signal to the Whiteman. Everybody will know it was us who needed a head, so the radius of the investigation would be zeroed to us once the incident was reported. But it would be different if the victim came from us. It would be us who were expected to make the report, but since it was our thing we would handle it like ours."

We all concurred to his ideas. When it was asked from whose family we should get the head, a straight answer came from me: from Nduka's, the family of Mrs. Nkechi. None of the cabinet contested that. For one thing, none of them had a personal stake in the family; moreover, the family had the two heads we were looking for: Nduka, Nkechi's husband, and that of their only child. What else made the family vulnerable was that they were poor and had no threat in the form of a person who would protest for them.

I reassured the king again that it wasn't the ghost of Nduka that came in the form of the winged animal to hunt us. All his curses and the promises of revenge were natural from a person dying in a similar circumstance like him. None of them meant anything. I then told him that it would be better if we listened to the story of those two wailing woman outside the court before we made our decisions. He agreed.

The stories of the two women were similar to that of the couple that came earlier. The only difference was that one of the women admitted seeing the back of the gigantic bird as it flew away with her son. When we asked her to describe the bird, her details matched those of Mrs. Nkechi. The king then asked them when the incident took place; there was fifteen minutes interval between the times the first woman lost her child to that of the second. The king asked the first woman, who suspected that her son was missing, why didn't she quickly run to report? She answered that she had to take her time to search around before she came to report. The king dismissed the two women, promising them that he would dispatch warriors immediately to hunt down the bird and bring back their children.

Immediately they left; the king turned to me. "Are you telling me that this wasn't Nduka in action?"

"I don't think so, your highness," I replied.

"Why did it appear to his wife first if not to inform us that his torture has come?"

"I think it was a mere coincidence, your highness. Somebody must be the first person to see the bird. So I think there is not much deal that it was her."

The king kept quiet.

"Your Highness," Ojimba broke the silence, "I think we should talk on how to hunt down the creature."

"You are the chief of my security, arrange that with the warriors." The king waved dismissingly to him.

"Should we report to Whiteman?"

"Not until we know the root of the attack. I have to consult the native doctor," the king replied.

As I went home that day, I wondered whether or not the king's speculation was true. The thought gave me a ghost pimple. If that was true, I knew that I was vulnerable in a unique way. Two of my kids from the different wives of mine were in the age boundary in which the bird attacked. But the major reason was the role I played to make sure he was the victim of the sacrifice. I hated him, I knew I did. Ever since he married the woman of my lust, he was my targeted enemy. I had asked Nkechi to be my third wife after I watched her taking her bath but she refused. She rejected my wealth and influence for that wretched man. Ever since then

I had been looking for a way to break the marriage but to no avail. When the opportunity came, my plan was that after his death I could marry her, but it never happened. His death and that of her son broke her. At first I thought that she would recover but it wasn't to be so. She took to drink, and each day her beauty faded with the shadows. I still wonder what really got hold of me to lust for her that much, judging with her present shape.

Tomorrow's bombshell was more terrifying. The king had consulted the village native doctor. He confirmed that that bird was Nduka on a revenge mission. They had wanted to stop him with a sacrifice but his spirit was tough. In the form of the bird, it came and fiercely devoured the native doctor — rippled away his heart. It later laid the heart on the top of his grave. Our problem returned in more complex form.

*

Civilization flourished at this fallen town in the 1800s. From artefacts we excavated, we saw strong evidence to this. Moreover, some architectural structures still remained intact. Moving to the middle of the town, we located a series of artefacts that suggested royalty; we think that the town was planned in such a way that the king lived at the centre of his realm. There were altars there and on a particular one, with our investigations, showed that human sacrifice was conducted.

What led to the fall of the city was still a puzzle to us, but from all we could see there was no attempt made by the cities around to re-occupy the land. Even now, the indigenes of the nearby cities refuse to go to the land. None of those we interviewed had any reason beyond that it was a custom they grew to know.

There were government efforts to turn the fallen town into a tourism centre, but the indigenes of the nearby cities opposed this, claiming that according to tradition it was a cursed city. Any effort to do that would regenerate the emergence of a blood thirsting mystic bird killing all their children. I don't believe in such a myth, and who knows for how long the government would keep listening to them?

THE GAME OF AIDS

I am Maria, a mother of two; a widow and a victim of HIV/AIDS. Don't rush to a conclusion by saying, "Yeah, this is nice for those of you who are unfaithful to their husbands." I am not going into self-defence, but as much as possible I have to be plain with the facts. The HIV virus in my body was a gift from my husband. He was the first person to have carnal knowledge of me and he remained the only one.

But will this make me call him the betrayer of our matrimonial vow? I doubt that. But I wouldn't vow for his innocence too. Events shrouding my present life are complicated and blurred.

The day my husband discovered that he had the virus he came home crying like a baby. He was sick for some time; we thought it was malaria, a usual sickness here. We Igbos in the Eastern part of Nigeria live in a tropical zone. Our climate highly favours mosquitoes. Iba, our word for malaria fever, is a common sickness, the first illness anybody suspects if someone is sick. In eighty percent of cases that diagnosis is right.

My husband used local herbs to treat his suspected malaria. Since the time we married that was the kind of drug he preferred to use to cure his illness. It always amused me. I couldn't comprehend how an educated man of his kind would prefer indigenous medications over scientific ones. It looked stupid, a fetish. I tried to persuade him, when we were newly married, to abandon that archaic behaviour but he refused. He insisted that this method worked for him and that there was no need to change. Besides, he said that western drugs have no effect on him, taking it was like swallowing chalk. Later, I discovered that the real reason was his experience with chloroquine tablets as a child. He fell sick and his mother brought the tablets for him. The drug reacted negatively on his body. He nearly went blind and there was a tumour growing on his head. Then there was the itching all over his body. He hardly slept, and this lasted for days. Ever since then he has had an aversion and phobia towards anything he classifies as a western drug. Anyway, from the moment I knew of this story, I allowed him to live with his bias.

On this particular occasion, he took the herbs for up to three weeks and nothing positive happened. Instead his health was deteriorating. I became afraid. I had fear because, even though he was often sick, at least once every other month, the infirmity never lasted beyond a week, but the longevity of his current illness was outrageous. People said that being often ill was normal for AA blood groups. I don't know how truthful that is. But I often used it as a consolation whenever he was not well since he was an AA.

When I saw that this case was an anomaly compared to the other times he was ill, I persuaded him to try an alternative method and go to a hospital for treatment, but he refused. He insisted that it must be herbal drugs or nothing. What he then did was to abandon the herb he was using and jump to another. When it became clear to him that one wasn't working, he always did that. About a month later, he saw that nothing good was coming from his herbs and he began to see sense.

I was cooking in the kitchen; it was early morning on our market day. He came and leant against the wall, his hands tucked in the pocket of his blue jeans. His face looked like that of a hungry child in an OXFAM advert. He said, "I think my malaria has out-grown the power of herbal drugs."

I managed to withhold my laughter because I knew that his health was pitiable and that his mood was not a joking matter. The same day he went to St. Jude's, our local hospital, to see a doctor. The hospital wasn't far away from our house. I would have followed him to the hospital but I didn't because I needed to buy foodstuffs from our market Eke. Among us women, we fondly call Eke day a "holy day of obligation" because nobody dare miss going unless you are planning a hunger strike for your family.

Because I knew his health condition, I was afraid that he would be admitted into hospital. Doctors are notorious for doing that kind of a thing. "Hello friend, I am sorry we have to put you in bed for a couple of days," and that is the end of it.

In the market I rushed, buying things as quickly as I could to get home fast. I needed to meet him in the hospital. If he got admitted and I wasn't there, rumours would spread. People would call me all sorts of names and would invent something about me to use as the topic of gossip. Some would say I was too laid back. Others would say that I was wicked, a witch who killed her husband to inherent his wealth, so that I could enjoy life with my secret lover.

I was unloading my purchases from the market into the food store in my kitchen when he came home. He was downcast, crying and wailing just like a kid. My heart somersaulted. I was dumbfounded and confused. I didn't know what to do or the right words to say. I just stood there like a statue staring at him with my mouth agape. But quickly I regained my composure, rushed to him and held him tight. By then tears were freely rolling from my eyes. I kissed him passionately on the lips and then I kissed his salty tears. Later, I fetched a handkerchief from my bag and began to dry his tears. We were like that until he began to pull himself together. He took the handkerchief from me and started to dry my tears.

"Honey," he said with a strange voice, a voice too strange to be his.

I just nodded and looked at him.

"I am finished."

"What is it?" I implored in a calm voice. "We can solve it together."

He looked at me and shook his head.

"So you no longer trust me?" I asked.

"I do."

"Then tell me."

"I am HIV positive."

I took a sharp breath. I felt like collapsing. Confused thoughts flowed through my mind. I am not a health expert but I knew many things about HIV. Who on earth doesn't know? Just turn on your radio or TV for a few seconds and adverts about it will flow like a river. Walk around the village and you will see things posted on different billboards. Go to our Mothers' meetings and you receive a series of lectures on the same thing. In fact, I started hearing about this disease when I was eight. That was when one of my classmates came to school with a used condom. We were playing with it, we thought it was a balloon, until our teacher stumbled upon us and told us. I nearly vomited my intestine out that day. That was many years ago but now even a child in the womb knew about the presence of the disease.

I wondered how, when and why he contracted the disease. Was I also a victim? How about our two children? Who is safe and who are the victims? I knew that he had his own clipper, so the chance of contracting the disease through hair cut in a salon was unlikely. He was such a meticulous man that he would be the last person to have a haircut using a public clipper. Once he discovered that his clipper had been stolen by I-don't-know-who, he abandoned having a haircut until he got a new clipper. And as far as I knew, he had never been sick enough to need a blood transfusion. He himself had an aversion to that. I suspected that it was part of the influence he got from his church before becoming an atheist. Should I really call him an atheist? I think his belief is somewhere in-between theism and atheism. Why I say this is because if atheism means a person who doesn't believe in the existence of God, then that wasn't him because he does believe. Yet if theism meant someone who worships any supreme being, then that wasn't him; because he worshipped no such one. Deep within me, I knew that the only way he could have contracted the virus was through sexual intercourse; an extra marital affair. I felt stabbed in the heart. I felt betrayed.

It was like he was reading my thoughts.

"I know you no longer trust me," he said.

I tried to say something but I was so confused I lost the power of speech.

"Yeah, you are right in whatever you are thinking. But all I want you to know is that I was not cheating on you. I never did and I will never do it."

"So tell me how you got AIDS?" I asked, sobbing. "Tell me."

He kept quiet for a while before responding, "Honest, I don't know."

"So what are you talking about? You are taking me for a kid?"

"I am not telling you this so that you will believe me. I know that there is no way you can believe me. If I was in your shoes, I would react the same or even more aggressive than you. But being frank with you, I have never cheated on you. I think something is mixed up somewhere. I will figure it out soon."

Immediately he said that, he left me and went straight to where we kept our condoms. For the past five years, we have been using condoms when we make love especially during those times I knew I was at risk of becoming pregnant. We had agreed that we were already content with our kids. We no longer needed more. A decision we believed would leave us with the resources to take good care of the two children that we had. I wanted to stop him and ask what he was going to do with the condoms but I was angry and annoyed.

When he left, I was thinking about whether he had told the truth or not? Was he actually telling me the truth or was this just a defensive mechanism? One of those mechanisms my mother always tells me that men are pretty good at. Was he evading his responsibility? Or was he telling me as much as he knew himself?

I have many reasons to believe him. For the past ten years I have been living with him, I have had no cause to suspect him. You may say that he was playing it smart but I don't think so. He had been as open and as truthful with me as a kid. Most of the time, it was I who hid little secrets from him. His innocence was charming and disarming. Things he told me; I knew that if I was in his shoes I would never have done the same. For instance, I still remember a shocking truth he revealed to me. His younger brother married and when in the course of the marriage he was unable to get a child, he went for a test. To his shock, he was infertile. He then embarked on treatment that ranged from orthodox medicine to African traditional medicine, but none yielded fruit. At a certain time in his life it became clear to him that the situation had come to stay. But what he feared most was the gossip that was spreading. He was too ashamed to face it.

To save the situation, he agreed with his wife that they would find another man to impregnate her. They decided that my husband was going to be the man. This kind of situation traditionally is kept away from women except the person directly involved. It is believed that women don't keep secrets. But my husband went against the tradition because of his love for me, not minding the consequences. He told me. If it was left for him to decide he would have done it, but he said that he couldn't do it without my consent. When he told me that I was shocked because I knew the tradition and the risk he was taking by telling me. I was also shocked because deep within me I knew that if a similar situation had befallen me, I wouldn't have told him. But there he was sincerely seeking my opinion. I pitied his brother and his wife but I was a jealous type, I can't bear seeing another woman sharing my husband with me. I told him to refuse and he did. It nearly tore our extended family apart. They accused my husband of intending to inherit his brother's property if his brother died, but he stood his ground because of me. How could such a man cheat on me?

At night that day neither of us ate. It was like we were mourning somebody. We lay on our bed staring at the ceiling, not talking. Later he broke the silence.

"I am suspecting that the disease came from the condoms we have been using," he said.

"What do you mean? Condoms are meant to prevent AIDS and not to spread it. Have you forgotten?"

"Theoretically, you are quite right; but practically, you are wrong."

"What do you mean?"

"What I mean is that many things are going on at present in the name of technology."

"How?"

"Do you know the reason why my younger brother was infertile?"

"No. I thought he was born like that?"

"No. I am sure he wasn't. When he was growing up, he impregnated his girlfriend twice. But they aborted the child."

"Then what happened?"

"They went to a peace keeping mission in Rwanda. During that period, they ate canned food supplied to them."

He kept quiet

"And then?" I asked.

"It was later discovered that all who ate the food became infertile."

"I don't believe this. What does a person gain by making them so?"

"This is a similar question I have been asking myself. Okay. Have you not heard about a certain kind of belt that reduces people's sperm count?"

"What kind of belt?"

"My friend had a problem with impregnating his wife. He then went to see a doctor to know the reason. The doctor asked him to show him the belt he was wearing. To his utmost surprise, the doctor said that his problem was as a result of the belt. They forced the buckle of the belt open, and something like a magnet fell out. The doctor said that it was the reason. It was a discovery they had recently made regarding the belt. The magnetic substance reduces sperm count."

"Frankly, I have heard a similar rumour before, but I never believed it."

"Better believe it now. It is not a rumour. It is a fact."

"So what do you think about our own case?"

"I think it is the same. I took the condoms to the hospital. They ran a series of tests on them, but they all came back negative. You must remember that we have been using these condoms for many years now; nobody can tell when we picked the one that has caused this trouble. The doctor said that my suspicious could be right."

"Or wrong?"

"Honey, please believe me. I am telling you the whole truth."

He died later. I did take my children to the hospital so that we could check our status. Luckily, they were negative but I was unfortunate to be diagnosed positive. Immediately after his death, many versions of the story emerged as to how he contracted the disease. Some said he was sleeping with his boss, others said it was his secretary. Some even said he was bewitched with the disease. Some people believe that witches can transmit the disease. Whatever is the case I can't say, but one thing I know is that he has left me with many more questions than answers.

THE GREEN RACE

"It is my honour to introduce to you Professor Oliver Brown from Harvard University," Macdonald, the Chief Librarian of St. James Library, Ontario, Canada said, dabbing his face with a white handkerchief.

There was loud clapping. Oliver smiled, revealing his gapped teeth, and involuntarily touched his pointed nose. The light from the fluorescent tube glittered on his blonde hair and reflected on his blue eyes.

"St. James Library has the privilege of attracting eminent scholars around the world. And today, Professor Brown, the only historian that travelled with the astronomers who discovered the Green Race, will be talking to us about his new book, *The Green Race and the Rest of Us*. And of course, he will tell us what inspired him as a historian to become interested in space travelling."

Macdonald walked out from the dais, adjusted his black suit. He shook hands with Brown, whose chin could comfortably touch the centre of Macdonald's head should he lean towards him. They exchanged a grin. Brown mounted the rostrum.

"I thank the chief librarian and other administrators of this library for giving me this opportunity to speak about my new book, *The Green Race and the Rest of Us*. I would like to begin with a passage where I described this people."

Brown flipped through the pages of the black hardcover book; the ruffling of the pages of the book was the only sound in the hall.

"I will be reading from page twelve," Brown said. "'We

were on planet Mars'," he began. "'On the fifth day of our arrival, Bob was trying to calculate the velocity of light from the sun and to compare it to what we have on the earth when he noticed the movement of two beings. He immediately contacted all of us through his radio. With our telescopes, each watched the two beings. They were a male and a female. They looked like a couple, a lovebird with the usual public display of affections. They were naked with a green body colour. The male was about six inches tall, muscles all over the body, a King Kong of a sort, or more like one suffering from the excess dosage of steroid pills. The head had wide eyes and a jaw like a lion. The head was twice the size of any regular head seen on the earth. Its chest bulged, with arms and feet like an athlete. In between his legs was his manhood, which looked like an insult to the massive body. It hung feeble, mal-developed and shrieked.'"

Loud laughter ran through the crowd.

"'The male had hairy legs and arms,'" Brown continued, "'the hair on the legs started from the knee and ended on the ankle. The hair on its body wasn't like animal hairs, a monkey or a chimpanzee, and it wasn't typically human either. It was tall, thick and erected like thorns. The hair in its arms ended at the elbow too. The rest of the body was as smooth as a mirror. Whereas the female, shorter than the male, was about four inches tall. Green bodied too. She had no significant muscle that differentiated her from human, but the head, just like that of the man, was big, eyes and jaws in a scary proportion. Her breast, as if it was compensating for the tiny pin-like penis of the man, was as large as a mature pawpaw. The female had no hair apart from her genital area where the thorny hair clustered like trees in a savannah.'"

Brown, raised his head. "Off from the book," he said, and

106

smiled, "I wondered how the man gets the job done on such a grassy thorny route."

There was a chuckle of laughter among the audience.

"I will drop the book for a moment and talk about the points I raised in the book which some people find controversial. I will of course read some extracts as we move on in this discourse," Brown said. He reached for a glass of water resting on the edge of the lectern and sipped.

"What interested me most in writing a book about this people," Brown began, "is that I don't want us in the West to make the same mistake our fathers made in Africa. Even up till now, Africans use that as an excuse to heap on us all the blames of all their misfortunes, underdevelopment and misadministration. Of course, this is not a book about Africans. I am not sure if I can write any about them. I love beauty, I love purity. I can't see myself writing about those deplorable themes like wars, hunger, disease, bad government and those subjects we know are synonymous to the third world. In fact, one day I was about to eat my favourite chicken pie and my wife brought some flyers, I can't remember by what charity organisation now but it contained this picture of three African children, a boy and two girls in rags, with gaping mouths without teeth inside, running noses, standing behind a stream a brownish colour, my hunger ceased. OXFAM has a lot of those pictures. Donate to them. Those people are terribly hungry."

The audience laughed.

"I am not a racist. And I don't want to sound like one. A lot of my colleagues in the history department of Harvard University are black people and I get along with them pretty well. But I am a pragmatist. So I am not economical with the truth most often. And I find that it is a problem with some people who are already a closed book, if you know what I mean. Anyway this is not the crux of the matter. We are here to discuss the Green Race and how we are going to relate with them, especially now we have just seen them and we have made minimal contacts with them.

"And this brings me straight to the controversial point in my text. I will read from the book."

Brown flipped through the book again.

"I will be reading from page one hundred and fifty," Brown said. "'At the core of our relationship with the green race,'" Brown began reading, "'is whether we should classify them as human beings or something close to our species. If we call them humans, it means we have to admit them as those protected by human right. But if we see them as something close to us, we can then treat them in a similar way we treat monkeys or chimpanzees or in a more dignified way.'"

Brown raised his head and sipped from the glass of water beside him.

"How can we establish the humanness or lack of it in this being?" Brown asked. "In other words: what is the distinguishing criterion that makes our race unique and different from others?

"I will discuss a few instances that I covered in my book. The rest you can read up.

"Excuse me," Brown said as he coughed.

"Physiologically," Brown began, "we differ from them. I am not talking about colour. It is an insignificant thing to bother about. To be fair, the green species aren't monsters but they are a twin to them."

There was an uproar of laughter from the audience.

"I will show you something now," Brown said, stepping out from the rostrum.

Beside where Brown stood was a rectangular glass table.

On its top was a laptop and a projector. Brown walked to the table, drew the laptop nearer and began typing.

"Let's see how they look. I mean our lovely Green Race," Brown said, smiling.

"Aww..." came from the audience.

"They are cute, I bet you," Brown added amidst laughter.

Laughter echoed from the audience too.

Brown clicked his PC, frowning. Then his face lit with a smile.

"Here we go."

"Oh gosh...!" The audience screamed as the image from the projector popped up on the white board in front of them. Some were laughing.

"I said it. Look at their eyes bulging out, and their jaws and the spade-like teeth, the slanted tongue like a reptile's, the muscle, its rigidity. Watch the tough thorny hairs. Don't they look like Cthulhu, that mysterious horror god?"

The audience rolled out in laughter.

Brown went back and stood beside the lectern, arms folded across his breast.

"As you can see," Brown said when the noise abated, "they aren't like us physically. Anatomically, the major area of contention is their DNA. Scientists have argued that if their genetic makeup is the same as ours, we are left with no other option but to call them human because it means we can cross breed together. But recent research conducted by Prof Lucas Lawrence from the Genetic Engineering department of Swansea University in Wales, showed that their DNA is an isotope to that of humans. This was further confirmed by independent research by the renowned scientist Mathew Hob of Harvard University.

"Beyond this fact is the debate on whether or not the isotope qualifies them as humans. Some scientists argue that they are us because of the isomer but I beg to differ. I see the assertion as a fallacy. For me, you are either human or you are not. Anything apart from this is a contradiction. To be human you have to be human in everything. Look at the black race and the white race, beyond the skin, the rest is the same anatomically. But with the green race, it is another ball game. The difference in the isotope is a great deal, a big leap from humanness.

"Research is still in progress at Harvard University. Scientists are trying to see if their semen can fertilize the ovary of a human egg. I doubt whether it will ever be possible because of the instability in their DNA when it reacts with ours, which is its isomer. But assuming it ever happens, that fertilization can take place, I assure you that the result will be something that has every quality apart from humanness.

"It is because of this that I assert in my book – let me read it from the book directly," Brown said.

Brown mounted the lectern. He turned the pages of the book.

"On page three hundred and five I wrote: 'Empathy is necessary but shouldn't come in when a clear and precise logic should work. And we shouldn't be afraid to categorically state things the way they are. The idea that the Green Race is human is but a mad logic of individuals suffering from the syndrome of white guilt, which the media are currently spreading among the white folks.'"

Brown lifted his face up and whispered into the mike, "I bet you this is the worst period of time to be a male white guy."

The audience thundered with laughter.

"Anyway the above paragraph I just read is the most misquoted from my book and often placed out of context with a lot of people calling me a racial bigot beclouded under white male privilege.

"I don't know what they mean by that anyway."

The audience laughed.

"But whatever, in science and in academic scholarship, personal sentiment should be left out for pure facts. Science is not myth, a made up story like fiction. I am not saying that fiction is not relevant," Brown whispered in the mike.

People laughed.

"Sure they are. My best friend is a writer. I don't want him to end our friendship."

There was a roll of laughter from the audience again.

"I will add that I am not a big fan of religion but my colleague, John Smith, in the theology department of Harvard University, has raised an issue as to whether or not the Green people have souls. He thinks they have none, since there is no place in the Bible where their existence is mentioned. For them to be human, he said, they should have their own Christ who died for them.

"But we all know that we don't have two Christs."

Brown took a glance on his wrist watch.

"To sum everything up, since time is against us," Brown said, "I have two recommendations to make regarding our relationship with them.

"I will read from page four hundred of the book."

There was silence in the hall as he searched for the right page.

"'I propose,'" Brown began, "'that since they are sub-human but above animal, we should:

"'Open a charity trust fund for them for clothing and other related matters. And then we should attempt and try to civilize them as much as we can by giving them language and culture, assuming they can learn it. And that in return, we should exploit the mineral resources of their planet. Part of the profit will certainly be devoted to the development of their planet.'"

Brown lifted his face from the book to look directly at the audience.

"Let's be fair," Brown said, "even if we leave the minerals unmined, they wouldn't mine it because it is of no value to them."

As the audience laughed, he read amidst their cheering;

"'Or: B: we should leave them as they are so that tourists can go and watch them as wildlife.'"

Clapping and more cheering vibrated in the hall.

"Lest I forget," Brown said when the clapping had subsided, "let me answer one major question I get whenever I discuss my book with an audience, and that is why, as a historian, I am interested in space travelling. Macdonald hinted at that earlier.

"My honest answer is that modern historians are not only meant to archive important events when they occur, as our predecessors did, but they should also work hard in creating these histories.

"Thank you for tonight."

There was a standing ovation for him.

Parallel Universe Publications

INTO THE DARK by Andrew Jennings
ISBN: 978-0-9935742-5-2

TOUGH GUYS by Adrian Cole
ISBN: 978-0-9935742-2-1

CLASSIC WEIRD 2 selected by David A. Riley
ISBN: 978-0-9932888-4-5

OTHER VISIONS OF HEAVEN AND HELL by Jessica Palmer
ISBN: 978-0-9935742-1-4

A SAUCERFUL OF SECRETS by Andrew Darlington
ISBN: 978-0-9935742-0-7

THE WINTER HUNT AND OTHER STORIES
by Steve Lockley & Paul Lewis
ISBN: 978-0-9932888-9-0

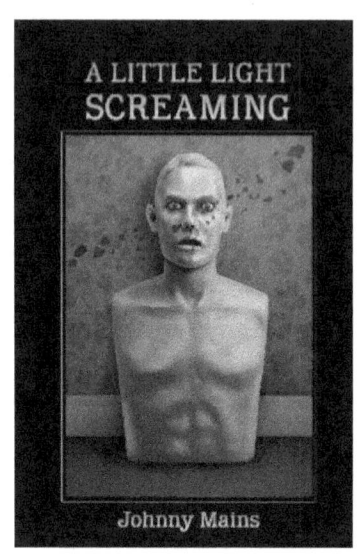

A LITTLE LIGHT SCREAMING by Johnny Mains
ISBN: 978-0-9932888-5-2

ENGLAND 'B': 90 MINUTES OF HELL by Richard Staines
ISBN: 978-0-9932888-7-6

AND NOBODY LIVED HAPPILY EVER AFTER by Kate Farrell
ISBN: 978-0-9932888-8-3

FISHHEAD; THE DARKER TALES OF IRVIN S. COBB
ISBN: 978-0-9935742-4-5

KITCHEN SINK GOTHIC: Selected by David and Linden Riley
ISBN: 978-0-9932888-3-8

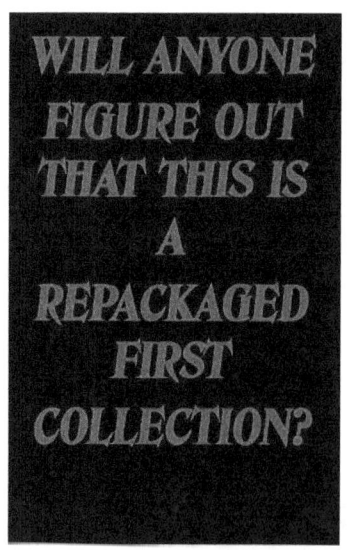

WILL ANYONE FIGURE OUT THAT THIS IS A REPACKAGED FIRST
COLLECTION? by Johnny Mains
ISBN: 978-0-9574535-7-9

BLACK CEREMONIES by Charles Black
ISBN: 978-0-9574535-5-5

HIS OWN MAD DEMONS:
DARK TALES FROM DAVID A. RILEY
ISBN: 978-0-9574535-8-6

THEIR CRAMPED DARK WORLD by David A. Riley
ISBN: 978-0-9574535-9-3

THE HEAVEN MAKER AND OTHER GRUESOME TALES
by Craig Herbertson
ISBN: 978-0-9932888-2-1

GOBLIN MIRE by David A. Riley
ISBN: 978-0-9574535-4-8

THINGS THAT GO BUMP IN THE NIGHT
selected by Douglas Draa and David A. Riley
ISBN: 978-0-9574535-6-2

CLASSIC WEIRD selected David A. Riley
ISBN: 978-0-9574535-3-1

MOLOCH'S CHILDREN by David A. Riley
ISBN: 978-0-9932888-1-4

Check our website:

http://paralleluniversepublications.blogspot.co.uk/

www.ingramcontent.com/pod-product-compliance
Lightning Source LLC
Chambersburg PA
CBHW061138200626
46817CB00016B/1972